Barbary Coast Gundown

A brush with outlaws leads to the chance meeting of Matt Sutton and Diana Logan with Percy Wilberforce, a private detective from London. He recruits the pair to help him rescue an English countess abducted in the notorious Barbary Coast district and thought to be in the harem of a Chinese tong leader.

A bloody riot in Chinatown, a vicious street gang and a showdown with the tong leader and his hatchetmen all lay in wait for Matt and Diana.

Barbary Coast Gundown

JAMES GORDON WHITE

A Black Horse Western

ROBERT HALE · LONDON

ISBN-10: 0-7090-8153-7
ISBN-13: 978-0-7090-8153-1

Robert Hale Limited
Clerkenwell House
Clerkenwell Green
London EC1R 0HT

Typeset by
Derek Doyle & Associates, Shaw Heath
Printed and bound in Great Britain by
Antony Rowe Limited, Wiltshire

To
Shirley Eaton
The model for the blonde
heroines in my books and
past movies

CHAPTER ONE

California. Land of new lives, hopes, and opportunities. It had taken nigh on to a year to reach it, but Matt Sutton and Diana Logan had finally done so. There had been many obstacles along the way, mainly from Matt's past, but now all that would change. No one knew him here, and that was just how he wanted it. Other men had put their pasts behind them successfully in California, and that was what he full intended to do.

Matt wasn't a shootist or really an outlaw. He was a West Texas cowboy who had fallen into bad company in his youth, and had paid the price with a prison sentence. Diana had waited for him, and had then convinced him that California was the place to begin their lives anew. His wild oats sown, now at twenty-eight, Matt was a much wiser and more sober man.

Tall, tanned, ruggedly handsome and muscularly lean, with straight brown hair, and alert grey eyes, he looked strong yet personable. His clothes were simple and comfortable: dove-grey, flat-crowned hat, red bandanna, blue workshirt, faded denim jacket and pants, scuffed half-boots, and a low-slung, holstered Colt .45 on his gunbelt that looked very lethal and well used.

In contrast, his lady companion looked and dressed like a thoroughbred. Diana Logan was an exquisite beauty, with large, wide-spaced blue eyes above high, explicit cheekbones, classic nose, softly moulded lips, firm chin, and flowing golden hair that framed her delicate features. At twenty-six she looked no more than nineteen, and her clothes emphasized her stunning, willowy and statuesque figure.

A long, narrowly folded white scarf wrapped her slender neck, while a thin, white cotton shirt fit like a glove, as did a short, black leather jacket and matching riding skirt that spanned her slim hips smoothly and clung to her taut thighs. Black gloves, matching flat-crowned hat with a silver hatband and thin chin cord, and knee-length, stovepipe, high-heeled riding boots, completed her outfit.

Uprooted from her genteel East Texas mansion in bayou country by the late war's aftermath, the Reconstruction, that bled the states of the Southern Confederacy white, Diana had travelled to the south-west frontier territories of New Mexico and Arizona where she'd become a gambler, and had met Matt Sutton. Texans and Southerners in a territory that had held mainly Union sympathies during the war and still begrudged the Confederate invasion from Texas under Colonel John R. Baylor and its brief occupation, they had a common bond and enjoyed each other's company. Later, she stuck by Matt when he was sent to Yuma prison for stage-coach robbery. That was the past, and they now faced the future with hope.

The sleepy desert town of Los Angeles had not seemed a place to settle, so they were drifting north to the 'Babylon on the Pacific', San Francisco, where it was said fabulous fortunes were made and lost in the high-class casinos around Nob Hill and also the low-class ones on the fabled Barbary Coast. There was a steady supply of money streaming in daily from not only lucrative ship-ping, with imported goods from countries all over the Pacific, but also miners from the not too distant gold fields.

Matt and Diana had agreed they wanted to settle down to a life of ranching, though at the moment that would take more money than they had between them. Matt had insisted he would earn the money through ranch work, but both knew it would take a long time to do so. Perhaps he would find a better, money-earning (honest, of course) opportunity in San Francisco.

Because of Matt's objections Diana had not said any more but she kept her brief black gambling costume, and when the time was right she would again broach the subject with a much firmer atti-tude. Her Aunt Harriet, whose husband had been a riverboat gambler, had taught Diana as a child how to handle a deck of cards. It had been solely for amusement, until Harriet's death during the Reconstruction. Since then cards had become a business, and she felt confident that she could win the necessary money for a small ranch and live-stock. In spite of Matt's ingrained male pride, she saw nothing wrong in earning money for the both of them, especially when it was to be used to realize their dream.

The sun was sinking steadily in the west, moving beyond the horizon of the Pacific Ocean, which they could see in the distance from the hilltop they rode. It was time to start looking for a place to stop and eat, before pushing on to another spot where they would camp for the night. It was a precaution that the smart traveller always followed in Indian country, and even though California supposedly no longer had Indian trouble, it was still a wise proce-dure to follow. After all, there were plenty of Anglo and Mexican outlaws about, not to mention the various wild critters that could be drawn by the lingering odours of cooked food.

Ahead, about a mile away, smoke from a campfire rose above the pines. The two halted and exchanged questioning glances. Out in the wilder-ness folks could do as they wanted, with only their conscience (or lack of one) to guide them. Many a gullible traveller had lost his money and often his life to an outlaw, or someone desperate for a grub-stake to go prospecting for gold.

'Do you feel like a little company?' Matt asked drily.

Diana considered, then shrugged. 'Perhaps we will be invited to supper.' Then she added wistfully, 'It would be nice to go one night without cooking.'

'I like your cooking.'

'You'd better.'

'Yes, ma'am,' Matt said, straight-faced.

Exchanging smiles, they put their horses forward and headed down the slope.

It was the last stages of twilight by the time Matt and Diana had picked their way through a maze of towering pines and sat overlooking a camp from a wooded hillock. A large tent stood in a wide clearing; beyond was a wagon, and its unhitched but hobbled team grazed on the far side. A fat, balding man in evening clothes was seated at a folding table, complete with white tablecloth and silver-service set, while a stocky man in a butler's uniform poured a goblet of wine. To one side of the tent a hunk of unidentifiable meat was roasting on a spit above a cooking-fire. Matt and Diana stared dumbfounded at the incongruous sight before them. It was as if the men were in an elegant home instead of the wilderness.

'He certainly believes in all the comforts of home,' Diana observed.

'Yeah, the victuals oughta be right good.'

'By the size of that meat, there should be more than enough for guests.'

'I dunno, that fella looks to be a mighty big eater.'

'Shall we find out?'

'Why, sure.'

Reaching the edge of the clearing, the two halted and Matt hailed the camp. Western protocol dictated that a stranger did not enter a man's camp unless invited. The fat man called a cheery greeting, and they rode in and halted a short distance before the table. Again, Western manners decreed that a stranger stayed in the saddle until asked to step down.

'Please come and join me,' the greying, round-faced man, who looked to be late fifties, said amiably, his accent English. 'Boggs, kindly set two more places for dinner.'

'Right away, sir,' said the butler, a stern-faced man with slicked-down dark hair, who appeared to be in his late forties. He set the bottle on the table and turned away.

'Thanks,' Matt said, and the two dismounted. 'We'll tend to our horses and be with you directly.' He and Diana started to lead their horses off but froze in surprise when there was a sudden drumming of hoofs and five masked men charged into the clearing with guns drawn.

'Aw right, everybody hold it right where they are,' snarled their leader, a tall man in a red shirt and worn buckskin jacket, as he reined to a quick halt ahead of his group, only a few yards from Matt and Diana. 'This here's a stick-up,' he continued in a rough, gravelly voice. 'Raise your hands high and keep 'em like that, while we search for valuables.' Above his blue bandanna, his dark eyes played hotly over Diana. 'When we're done, you mount up and come with us, sugar. We got big plans for you.' The others' smirking voices eagerly agreed.

'Like hell, you do,' Matt said coldly.

'Shut up and get them hands up, mister.'

'My hand isn't going anywhere but down to my gun,' Matt said steely-eyed. 'And when I pull it I'm gonna kill every last one of you, starting with you, Red Shirt.'

'That's mighty brave talk for a fixing-to-be-dead man,' the leader scoffed.

'Please, I do so hate shooting,' the fat man said nervously and made to set down the goblet. His trembling hand bumped the wine bottle and upset it, spilling the red contents over the white table-cloth. 'Goodness, look what I have done. . . .' He picked up a large napkin and held it before him.

'Oh, my, sir,' the butler said in distress and uprighted the bottle.

'Hey, you two,' the leader shouted, as he and his group were momentarily diverted by the men's actions.

The distraction was all Matt needed. His draw was a lightning blur. 'Drop, Diana,' he said sharply. In swift sequence he blasted the leader from his saddle with a bullet through the centre of his forehead. Before Diana and the dead man hit the ground, Matt's next rapid shot tore through the left side of the second man's chest, crushing his heart, and hurled him, loose-limbed, from his mount, to sprawl against the third man, whose bullet went wild as his terrified horse shied away. Matt's third round slammed into the middle of his chest and dumped him backwards from his rearing horse.

Before Matt could fire again, the wine bottle shattered against the fourth man's masked face, showering glass in all directions. The man slumped sideways to the ground, dazed and moaning, his gun lost.

The fifth outlaw howled in agony as there was the report of a smaller gun and its slug broke his right shoulder. The heavy Colt fell from his numbed fingers and discharged harmlessly on striking the ground. Swaying in the saddle, the man clutched his bleeding shoulder and stared about, eyes huge above his mask, at the carnage.

Pistol trained on the wounded man, Matt threw a glance back at the tent and saw the fat man and the butler were approaching. The fat man held a smoking derringer, the butler a large carving knife.

'You took control of the situation quite admirably, sir,' the fat man said pleasantly. 'I cannot recall when I last saw such dexterity with a handgun.'

'Your distraction gave me the chance,' Matt said, and looked back at the two live outlaws.

'Allow me to help you up, miss,' the butler said solicitously and assisted Diana to her feet with his free hand.

'Thank you,' Diana said, then eyed the knife and asked lightly, 'Are you planning to take scalps?'

'Gracious, no, miss,' the butler said, appalled.

'Boggs is quite handy with a knife,' the fat man said.

'And throwing bottles, too,' Diana added.

'He learned his skill from the Gurkhas whilst we were serving on the north-west frontier,' the fat man informed the couple.

'Never heard of that tribe,' Matt said, still covering the outlaws, who were moaning and stirring. 'But we're from Texas, and don't rightly know much about the Indians in Oregon and Washington.'

Diana noted the men's bewildered expressions and said, 'I don't believe that is what he meant, Matt.'

'My error,' the fat man said affably, seeking to smooth over the misunderstanding. 'I forgot that America has its own north-west frontier. I meant the one in India. Khyber Pass, Afghanistan, and such.'

'Oh, *that* one,' Matt said sheepishly. 'Never was much on geography.' To change the subject, he asked, 'What do you want done with these two?'

'The nearest law is in San Francisco, which I calculate to be at least another day's journey,' the fat man said. 'I have pressing business there, and no time to spend filing charges, et cetera.'

'Us neither,' Matt said. 'Been a whole lot simpler if you'd shot a mite straighter, and Boggs here had used that knife instead of a bottle.'

'I had intended to,' the fat man said, and shrugged, 'but the man's horse moved.'

'Maybe it was for the best,' Matt said thoughtfully. 'Saves us the trouble of planting 'em. Never liked to work on an empty stomach.' He looked to Boggs. 'I don't mean to be telling you your business, but shouldn't you be checking on that meat? We don't want these jaspers' interruption to ruin dinner.'

Boggs turned enquiringly to his employer, who nodded. 'You shan't be needed here, Boggs.'

'Very good, sir,' Boggs said and strode away.

Matt glanced to Diana out of the tail of his eye. 'Why don't you take our horses off, and I'll be along to help you in a bit.'

'All right, Matt.' Diana gathered the horses' reins and led them away.

'Now to the business at hand,' Matt said gravely and stared with gimlet eyes at the wounded outlaws.

'Yes,' the fat man said with equal gravity, 'what *is* to be done with these brigands?'

CHAPTER TWO

Under the watchful eyes of Matt and the fat man, the two outlaws, whining about their wounds, slung their dead comrades across their saddles and then mounted their own horses.

Nose broken, cut face partly bandaged with his bandanna, the man who had been hit with the bottle gestured toward the nearby pile of rifles, knives, and six-guns. 'You ain't sending us off with no weapons?' he asked almost plaintively.

'You're lucky to be getting out of here alive at all,' Matt said harshly.

'Supposin' we meet up with a bear or mountain cat?' the man with the shoulder wound added uneasily.

'You outrun 'em or get et,' Matt said flatly. 'Now on your way, and take your trash with you for burying, and not anywhere near this camp.' His stern gaze swept slowly over the men's faces. 'If I ever see either of you again, I'll kill you on sight.'

Properly intimidated, the men rode from the clearing leading the dead men's horses. Matt and the fat man remained watching after them until they disappeared from sight. The fat man gave a heavy oral sigh and returned the derringer inside his dinner jacket, then smiled and said, 'The time has come for introductions. I am Percy Wilberforce, former colonel in Her Majesty's forces in India. Being retired, I only use the title on special occasions. Boggs was my batman – that is an orderly in your army – and he has been with me ever since. And you are?'

Matt holstered his Colt and put out his hand. 'Just plain Matt Sutton from West Texas.' They shook hands. 'And my lady is Diana Logan, a professional gambler by trade.'

'She appears the sort of young lady to whom a man would gladly lose his money.'

Matt grinned and added, 'You oughta see her gambling outfit.'

To Matt's and Diana's disappointment, the meat turned out to be wild boar. They sat looking glumly at their plates while Percy Wilberforce began eating with relish.

'Do not be bashful, my friends,' Wilberforce said between mouthfuls. 'The boar is most delicious. We've been dining on it for the last three days. Boggs has had much experience with it, since our days in India when the lancers went pig-sticking for sport.'

'I am sure he has,' Diana said politely, with a sideways glance to Matt.

'Meaning no disrespect to his cooking,' Matt said

uncomfortably, taking his cue from Diana, 'but, you see, down in Texas we don't eat *javalina.*'

'*Javalina?*' Wilberforce enquired.

'That's what we call wild pigs. They're mean customers, too. Run a man right up a tree, then dig at the roots to try and get him down.'

'May I ask the reason for abstaining from *javalina?*'

'The flesh is tainted by a fetid glan in its back,' Diana explained.

Wilberforce nodded. 'I am aware of the glan. However, Boggs knows a way to cook the boar in a pit and draw out all of the offensive secretions.'

'Pardon me, sir,' Boggs interjected. 'But I've been told that the Red Indians in the south-west also know that method.'

'Quite so,' Wilberforce agreed. 'Being a gourmet, I have studied the foods of different cultures.'

Matt was thoughtful for a moment, then nodded. 'Come to think of it, I have seen Indians eating *javalina,* but I was never of a mind to join them.'

'Shall we try it, Matt?' Diana said and cut a small piece of meat.

'Reckon so,' Matt agreed and followed her actions. 'Might just be we've been missing out on something good all these years.'

Overcoming their hesitation, the two sampled the meat and, surprised to find it quite edible, made the appropriate sounds of enjoyment. In fact, both even had a second helping. There was pleasant, mostly trivial dinner conversation, with

Wilberforce slyly directing questions to the couple and learning more about them than they did about him. Afterwards, Boggs brought out brandy and cigars.

'I apologize there is no drawing room to retire to, Miss Logan,' Wilberforce said, 'but it is just as well. I wish to discuss some matters with you both.'

'I sorta figured you had something on your mind, Mr Wilberforce,' Matt said. He waved away the offer of a cheroot. 'I don't smoke, chaw, gamble, or drink much. I tried 'em all, just so's I'd know what I was missing. Turned out I didn't figure I was missing much.'

'But Miss Logan is a gambler?' Wilberforce said with a questioning frown.

'Sure, but I don't play cards with her.'

'He doesn't like to lose,' Diana said lightly.

'It ain't the losing so much, as the thought of how my money coulda been better spent,' Matt admitted.

'Indubitably,' Wilberforce agreed and gave a throaty laugh. 'I have often felt that way myself. Mind you, my losses have always been small. Still, I dislike the idea of throwing money away, so to speak.'

'May I ask what you do for a living, Mr Wilberforce?' Diana said and smiled brightly.

'I am a private enquiry agent.' Noting their blank expressions, Wilberforce clarified the statement. 'That is what you would call a private detective.'

'Oh, like the Pinkerton Agency?' Diana said.

'Precisely, but I am in business for myself.'

'That's the only way to get rich,' Matt said. 'You

20

sure can't working for the other fella.'

Wilberforce nodded as Boggs lit his cigar with a match, then puffed it to life and considerately blew the smoke away from Diana.

'What are you doing out here?' Diana asked and waved a slim hand about at their wooded surroundings.

'I am on my way to San Francisco in the most inconspicuous way.' Wilberforce smiled and patted his girth. 'As you see, I am not built for crowded stagecoaches.' He laughed in self-mockery and continued. 'I wish to be incognito, and there are agents of certain parties who watch the new arrivals by ship, train and stagecoach.'

'Why the secrecy?' Matt asked.

'I am on a delicate mission that is two-fold.'

'Yes?' Diana prompted, her curiosity peaked.

'First, and most important, is to rescue a young British noblewoman who is being held against her will. To accomplish that I shall work secretly with the mayor's office to expose the city's corrupt politicians, particularly those who protect the Barbary Coast saloon owners and their ilk.'

'Sounds like you've got a hard row to hoe,' Matt drawled.

'Indeed. If I grasp your meaning correctly.'

'You must have a reason for telling us this, Mr Wilberforce?' Diana said politely but pointedly.

'You are on your way to San Francisco in search of employment. Since you will be strangers, I am assured that you are not secretly in the pay of anyone there.'

'That's right,' Matt said solemnly.

'I am authorized to hire agents to assist me. The pay will be quite lucrative in proportion to the risks you will encounter. Are you interested?'

Matt and Diana exchanged thoughtful glances. Both were tempted but cautious. 'We'd like to hear more before we decide,' Matt said. 'Particularly about the risks and pay.'

Wilberforce beamed. 'And so you shall.'

CHAPTER THREE

Matt and Diana listened intently while Percy Wilberforce related his tale.

'Two years ago Lord Hugh Stanton, the present Earl of Rossnere since his father's death earlier this year, and his bride, Lady Arabella, now Countess of Rossnere, came to North America during their world-trip honeymoon. The naïve young couple made the mistake of sight-seeing on the Barbary Coast with only a guide, instead of going with a party of tourists. The guide was unscrupulous. Lord Hugh was drugged, woke up to find he had been shanghaied aboard a ship to the Orient, and some months later managed to jump ship in Hong Kong. He returned to England in ill health and learned that his bride had also disappeared in San Francisco. Enquiries were made with no results, due to corrupt City politicians, as I mentioned earlier. Therefore, Lady Arabella must be found without any official help.'

'Do you know who might be holding her?' Diana asked.

'No ransom demands have been made through the British consulate, and it is believed that her abduction was for private rather than monetary reasons.'

'Somebody took a notion to have himself a high-class lady, huh?' Matt said.

'It appears that way.'

'But he can't rightly show her off, leastways not to many folks.'

'If it is the man whom I suspect, he is merely content with her company.'

'Who is that?' Diana asked.

'A certain saloon owner on the Barbary Coast has a silent partner, due to prejudice against Chinese, who is a tong leader and is known to have a harem of Caucasian women. Its exact location is unknown.'

'What is a tong?' Matt asked.

'For outward purposes, tongs are benevolent societies and mutual protection associations. In reality, they are bands of assassins and blackmailers that terrorize every Chinese community on the Pacific Coast. Their killers are called hatchetmen, but they use a variety of weapons.'

'Mean customers, eh?'

'They are mostly dangerous to other Chinese, as the tongs fear both Caucasian law and reprisals from the many prejudice groups in San Francisco, such as the hoodlums.'

'Hoodlums?' Diana asked, frowning in curiosity.

'A vicious street-gang made up of youths from teen years to early thirties who intimidate the Chinese, rob drunks, and generally bully anyone they can. They are best avoided if at all possible.'

Matt glanced to Diana. 'Sounds like San Francisco is an even livelier place than we expected.'

'Are you still interested?' Wilberforce asked and studied the couple sombrely.

'Seeing how we're going there regardless,' Matt said easily, 'we might as well know what we're getting into.'

'Stay out of waterfront saloons. They are where the riff-raff of the Pacific rim gather when ashore. And, whatever you do, do not drink anything, not even tea, or you will go to sleep and wake up shang-haied aboard a sailing ship.'

'Never had a hankering to go to sea,' Matt said drily. 'Reckon the Pacific doesn't look much differ-ent than the Gulf of Mexico down in Texas.'

'Then, of course, there are pickpockets, flim-flam artists seeking to part you from your money, card-sharks, and any other variety of large or petty crook that one finds in most cities.'

'You still haven't got around to telling what exactly you want of us,' Matt said, eyeing Wilberforce directly.

'Or what we will earn,' Diana put in.

'Very well,' Wilberforce agreed and drew on his cigar thoughtfully. After blowing a plume of grey smoke away from the table, he said, 'You, Miss Logan, will take a job as a gambler in the saloon where Lord and Lady Stanton met with misfortune. You will surreptitiously try to learn from the owner the location of his silent partner's harem of Caucasian women.'

'Suppose she can't and ends up in there herself?'
Matt said worriedly.

'There is always that risk,' Wilberforce said
candidly. 'But at the same time, you will also be
trying to learn the location from the tong leader
himself.'

'Just how do I do that?'

'There is bad blood among the various tongs.
Your man is trying to take over control of
Chinatown. As an extra precaution, he employs an
Irish bodyguard rather than a Chinese. You are to
remove that bodyguard any way you see fit and take
his place. Once you have gained the leader's confidence, you may be taken to where the harem is.'

'And then what?'

'Report to me, and we'll arrange the rescue.'

'Sounds simple enough,' Matt said wryly. 'Now
how about the pay?'

'Lord Stanton is a fair man. One thousand
pounds.'

Matt and Diana exchanged confused glances.
'Pounds of what?' Matt asked.

'That is British currency.'

'If it breaks down to anything like a thousand
dollars American,' Matt said, 'that's not enough.'

'A pound is equal to five of your American
dollars. So the price for your services would be five
thousand dollars, twenty-five hundred dollars
apiece. Is that more acceptable to the both of you?'

Matt and Diana were interested and very
tempted. 'Mind if we go talk it over between us?'
Matt asked.

'Certainly not, take all the time you wish.'

Leaving Wilberforce to his cigar and brandy, Matt and Diana rose from the table and walked out of earshot. 'Matt, it would mean our ranch without scrimping and saving for possibly years,' Diana said anxiously.

'Sure,' Matt allowed, 'but we haven't had any experience being spies or detectives. Those fellas sound pretty savvy. And don't forget, they are on their own ground. We're just a coupla strangers new to the big city.'

'Perhaps, but we are not simple. We have encountered men who were as mean or even meaner, and we are here to tell about it.'

'I'm thinking about you. Suppose things go wrong and you end up in that Chinaman's harem.'

'I am sure you will rescue me, as you have done in the past,' Diana said blithely.

'It has sorta become a habit,' Matt said and gave her an easy smile.

'Seriously, Matt, we may not have a chance for this much honest money again. It is not like we are giving up a better paying job that is waiting for us in San Francisco.' Matt nodded thoughtfully and, encouraged, Diana pressed on. 'I have faith in my ability and yours. And just think, we would be rescuing an English countess.'

'Guess we'd be doing a good turn, at that.'

'Then you agree?' Diana asked hopefully.

'You want this pretty bad,' Matt said, eyeing her evenly.

'I want us to be happy together on our own

ranch. Just the two of us and a herd of cattle.'

Though he was far from hen-pecked, Matt knew that when Diana had her mind made up it was near-impossible to deny her. Well, he wanted that ranch just as much, and they would be earning it by doing something good: rescuing a real noblewoman in distress. It sounded kinda romantic and out of a storybook, until he remembered that San Francisco and its inhabitants were real, and he was no white knight. His armour was more than a bit tarnished, to say the least.

Matt gave a heavy sigh of resignation, then put on his best smile and said, 'All right, let's go tell Mr Wilberforce that he's got himself a couple of hired hands.' Diana beamed and hugged him happily. Matt felt good all over and tried not to think about what lay ahead in San Francisco. He tried real hard.

CHAPTER FOUR

The remainder of the journey to San Francisco took a very leisurely three days, as Percy Wilberforce believed in briefing his new agents thoroughly. Matt and Diana were shown a photograph of Lady Arabella Stanton, an elegant beauty in her mid-twenties, and told to commit her image to memory. Since the photograph was not tinted, Wilberforce supplied her vital statistics: hazel eyes, auburn hair, and 5' 6".

Matt and Diana were told about Jake Bassity, owner of the Belle La Grande that was considered the biggest and best saloon on the Barbary Coast. His nearest competitor's saloon burned down the the previous year and its owner mysteriously disappeared, rumoured to have been shanghaied.

Fung Ching Doy, alias Little Pete, was not only Bassity's silent partner, but leader of the *Po Shin She* tong which was trying hard to gain control of all Chinatown, a section of nine city blocks containing an estimated thirty to forty thousand Chinese. A dandy possessing many diamond rings and gold watches, Little Pete changed jewelry several times a day and never wore the same suit two days in a row. Under his suits he wore a protective coat of chain mail, as did most other tong leaders and many hatchetmen.

From his years of card-playing in army barracks and gambling halls, Boggs fancied himself not only an expert with cards but a bit of a card-sharp. Nevertheless, he met his match with Diana, even when he tried various cheating techniques.

Wilberforce was pleased to see that Matt had not exaggerated his lady's skill. He was also impressed with her brief, black corset-like gambling costume, fishnet stockings and high French heels, all emphasizing her magnificent, statuesque figure and long beautiful legs. 'I have no doubt that Jake Bassity, a self-styled connoisseur of lovely women, will consider you, Miss Logan, an able asset to his establishment.'

Diana smiled sweetly. 'Thank you, Mr Wilberforce.' She gave a slight shiver as a cool sea breeze invaded their wooded camp. 'Now if you gentlemen will please excuse me, I would like to change into something warmer.' She rose and walked across the uneven ground to the tent as gracefully in her high heels as though she were barefooted.

Wilberforce looked across the table at Matt. 'Between the two of you I have every expectation that our venture will be brought to a swift and most satisfactory conclusion.'

'I sure hope so,' Matt said quietly.

Their last night on the trail was first spent reviewing their plans, then the group relaxed for a time. Idly shuffling cards, Diana asked, 'Mr Wilberforce, what made you take this case, as you call it? Surely there must have been other well-paying ones in London?'

'There were many, Miss Logan. But Lord Hugh's father, Lord Cyril, and I were cubs together in India. We rather lost touch after the service, then became reunited through a mutual friend, Dr Francis Buckland, a gourmet, surgeon, and naturalist, who founded the Society for the Acclimatization of Animals in the United Kingdom.'

'Sounds kinda high-falutin,' Matt said. 'What is it?'

'An organization devoted to increasing the nation's food supplies by breeding anything from kangaroos to bison in the fields of England.' Wilberforce smiled in pleasant remembrance. 'The society's annual dinner is always a most unusual treat, such as boiled elephant's trunk, rhinoceros pie, and whole roast ostrich.'

Matt and Diana exchanged queasy glances. 'It certainly does sound unusual,' Diana remarked.

'Then there are rather mundane courses, too. Breakfast servings are usually fieldmouse on toast.' Wilberforce paused as Diana abruptly turned ashen and let her cards spill about the tabletop in wild disarray. 'I do admit that is an acquired taste,' he said innocently.

Speechless, Diana tried to repress a shudder and

blot the mental image of eating a nasty, disgusting mouse from her mind's eye before it could cause her still-digesting dinner to rise up.

'So Lord Cyril got a hold of you when his son came home without his bride,' Matt said, noting Diana's distress and quickly changing the subject.

'Not immediately. He tried other avenues first, including your Pinkertons, but to no avail. I myself was engaged on another matter, and by the time I was free Lord Cyril had been stricken with pneumonia and died a short time later.'

'Why did father and son believe that you might accomplish what others here had not?' Diana asked and began gathering up her cards while still striving to keep her mind occupied on other things than mouse on toast.

'I have been to North America many times, and I also know the British consul in San Francisco. It was he who arranged for me to work with the mayor.'

'Kinda nice to have the right friends,' Matt commented.

'It is most important for someone in my line of work.' Wilberforce withdrew a large gold watch from a waistcoat pocket and checked the time. 'Now we should all retire,' he announced. 'Tomorrow will be a busy day, as the game begins in earnest.'

The four rode into San Francisco with a flood of traffic from travellers and morning trade wagons. Matt and Diana gawked like hillbillies at the largest city they had ever seen, with a population of over one hundred-thousand. There were storehouses, towers and steeples, court-houses, theatres, churches, hospitals, and more than one newspaper. Men and women wore city clothes, and many appeared to be Eastern finery from places such as New York City, St Louis, and even Paris. From Telegraph Hill, the city's highest point, a semaphore reported ship arrivals and, across the bay, steamers, freighters, and passenger ships lay at anchor.

At one of the many livery stables, they divested themselves of the wagon and horses. Plans were made to meet at noon at the Esterbrook Hotel, where Wilberforce would be staying, then Boggs went to secure lodgings for Matt and Diana in a hotel near Chinatown and the Barbary Coast.

'Your frontier clothes are quaint, but out of place here,' Wilberforce told the couple and then took them to various clothing stores.

Matt felt a mite uncomfortable in a three-piece suit, tie, and derby hat, but agreed he should try to fit in with the city folks. He did approve of the dressy clothes, hats, and other accessories that Wilberforce bought Diana with his expense money. He had never seen her in such finery, and, while she was stunning, the knowledge that it was done to lure another man secretly galled him. He wished he were able to buy her the things himself, for no other reason than to see the happiness in her face.

Afterwards the three took a ride through the Barbary Coast in a closed carriage for a look at the Belle La Grande in the daylight, as Diana would go there that night to meet Jake Bassity. Next they went through Chinatown for Matt to see that area.

It was noon when they met Boggs and learned that he had secured adjoining rooms in a once-stylish hotel in the desired location near Chinatown. Over lunch at an elegant restaurant the final details were set. From then on Wilberforce would remain in the background, but Matt and Diana could send a message to him at his hotel and both he and Boggs would occasionally be about to keep an eye on them. Wilberforce left to report his arrival to the mayor, and Boggs took Matt and Diana to their hotel, where they checked in separately.

The two settled into their rooms, then Matt went through the adjoining door into Diana's room and they passed the time in conversation until it was time for her to leave. He returned to his room to wait and try not to worry. That was easier said than done.

CHAPTER FIVE

In her new finery Diana Logan stood staring in over the swinging batwing doors at the interior of the Belle La Grande. Appearance was everything, and she wanted to know exactly where she was going without hesitation when she entered and not stand gawking like a farm girl at her surroundings while taking her bearings. She had worked in many saloons, some plain, others fancy by Western frontier standards, but the Belle La Grande had no equal. Huge, ornate, with an overabundance of gilt and glitter, it was considered the best on the Barbary Coast, with a clientele ranging from miners, sailors, local denizens, thrill-seeking tourists, to Nob Hill society.

A large stage with an orchestra pit below dominated the rear of the room. A maze of tables took up the centre, and a herd of waiters wove their way deftly through the narrow aisles with trays of drinks. A long mahogany bar with an equally lengthy mirror and large paintings spaced about it at intervals took up one side of the room, and a dozen barkeeps were busy serving a throng of customers lined the length of its brass rail. The opposite side of the room contained every type of gaming table imaginable, and people were throwing away their money hand over fist. Steps led up to a raised dining area that overlooked the main floor, and beyond were partitioned boxes for viewing the stage show in comfortable privacy. While no shotgun guard seated in a high chair (as in frontier saloons) was evident, Diana counted four burly men who looked very out of place in suits trying unsuccessfully to appear casual as they patrolled the various areas. She guessed there were more bouncers lurking about somewheres.

Drawing a deep, calming breath, Diana summoned her best cool and haughty demeanour and, clutching her reticule, pushed through the swinging doors. Not looking about her, she marched purposefully toward the gaming area. As she expected, a bouncer intercepted her just when she reached her destination.

'Where do you think you're going, girlie?' the man demanded roughly in a thick Irish brogue.

'Why to gamble, of course,' Diana replied, her tone and expression glacial, and eyed him as though he were an idiot child.

'No you ain't,' the brawny man responded, undaunted. 'Mister Bassity don't allow no unescorted "ladies" in here.' He jerked a thumb toward the swinging doors. 'Now git back out on the street where you belong, and don't be trying to take business away from our honest, hard-working girls.'

Feigning outrage, Diana stiffened and let even

more of the South come into her voice as she cried loudly, 'How dare you call me that, you petty, white trash cur.'

The man's bovine face flushed with anger. 'Now you're in for it, hussy.' He stepped forward menacingly. 'I'm tossing you out right on your backside.' He made to reach for her.

Long used to dealing with drunks and overly amorous cowhands, Diana stamped savagely on his instep and ground her French heel. Caught unawares, the man bellowed in pain and surprise, then drew back a meaty fist as he became aware of the onlookers laughing at him. With seemingly casual ease, Diana shifted off his foot and kicked him hard in the shin of his other leg. Again howling in agony, the bouncer did a brief dance of pain and sat down jarringly on the hardwood floor. The spectators erupted with laughter. Face beet-red with humiliation, the man gritted his teeth against the pain and angrily sought to rise. A stern voice halted him.

'All right, what's going on here, Rafferty?'

Diana turned to see a tall, rather beefy, dark-haired man in his middle thirties, well-dressed and somewhat handsome, with a drooping handlebar moustache, striding up from the direction of the raised dining area.

'Are you the proprietor, sir?' Diana demanded haughtily.

The fancy-dressed man halted before Diana, looked her up and down, plainly liking what he saw, then replied, 'I am. Jake Bassity is the name. How may I help you?'

'This "person" has insulted me,' Diana said, acting the indignant Southern belle.

'I was following your orders, Mister Bassity,' Rafferty said defensively and clambered to his feet. 'No unescorted "ladies" allowed.'

'That's right,' Bassity said to Diana.

'I am a professional gambler,' Diana stated coolly. 'I have gambled in saloons all over the West, and I have never before been refused entry.'

'Suppose you join me at my private table,' Bassity said charmingly, 'and we'll discuss the matter further?'

Diana pretended to consider, then favoured him with a bewitching smile. 'I would be delighted to do so, Mister Bassity.' She took his arm and let him escort her toward the raised dining area.

Being seen with a truly beautiful woman was always an ego-builder, and Jake Bassity revelled in the envious glances from the men at the tables they passed. He seated Diana at his table and sat across from her. 'Now then, Miss. . . ?'

'Logan,' Diana supplied, then purred, 'but call me Diana.'

'My pleasure,' Bassity said, staring into her large blue eyes, then added, 'Dixie suits you better. You are from that part of the country, I take it?'

'East Texas.'

'Why are you so far from home?'

'Gambling takes me all over.' Diana shrugged her slim shoulders. 'Besides, there is not much money in the South since the war.'

Bassity nodded. 'Yeah, there are a lot of

Southerners about at loose ends.' He eyed her evenly. 'I make it a rule that no ladies are allowed to gamble unless they work for me. I'm sorry but I can't make exceptions. I pay a weekly salary and a ten per cent commission on any winnings. Nothing if you lose, and that better not be too often. As far as the Law is concerned, I run an honest game. Cheat at your own risk. Get caught, and you're out on your ear.'

'There are some folks who don't have to cheat to win.'

'And you're one of them?'

'You'll find out . . . if I decide to take your offer.'

'I haven't made one yet.'

Diana smiled knowingly. 'But you will, Mister Bassity.'

'The name's Jake.'

Before Diana could speak, a man announced from the stage that the show was about to start. She looked over to see the stage where a man in a checked suit stood and noticed a tall, big-boned, cheaply attractive redhead in a dancehall outfit staring hard at her. The woman turned slowly and walked backstage as the man announced all gambling would cease during the show.

'That's my own rule,' Bassity said proudly. 'No distractions so the customers can enjoy the show without a bunch of noise.' Then he added slyly, 'It also gives them time for some serious, undisturbed drinking.'

'So they will hopefully be in the right mood to gamble more recklessly when the show is over,'

Diana said drily.

'That's often the case,' Bassity admitted with an equal dryness. 'Now how about some champagne?'

'Since I am not gambling tonight,' Diana said and gave a shrug, 'why not?'

Bassity grinned and signalled a waiter.

Diana had seen terrible stage acts before but most could not a hold a candle to those at the Belle La Grande, and as with most bad acts they seemed to go on interminably. The first was Emma, a small, frail-looking singer who screeched ballads at the top of her lungs. She was followed by the Dancing Emersons, two fat sisters who performed a classical dance, lumbering about the stage like a brace of elephants. Then came the main attraction: Big Molly in a comical condensed version of *Mazeppa* strapped to the back of a donkey. Diana could not fathom the act's popularity and, bored, thought how she would do the part with a horse. When the show mercifully ended, Bassity asked her opinion.

'I believe the part should be played serious and seductive,' she replied, 'as Adah Isaacs Menken originally did in her shocking pink tights.' She smiled and added, hoping to soften any unintentional insult, in case the comedy had been his idea, 'Ever since then, people have forgotten that the Mazeppa in Lord Byron's poem was a Tartar hero.'

'A supposedly naked woman is more interesting to see than a man . . . particularly if somebody like you were Mazeppa.'

'I'm a gambler not an actress,' Diana said simply.

'Too bad,' Bassity said wistfully, then pulled a fancy gold watch from a vest pocket and checked the time. Putting the watch away, he asked, 'How would you like to go to Chinatown with me?'

Careful not to leap at the chance, Diana frowned quizzically. 'Chinatown?'

'I have a large and important bet there.'

'Instead of here in your own saloon?'

'There are other things to wager on besides cards, dice, and the turn of a wheel. Since you're a gambling lady, you might want to place a bet yourself.'

'Perhaps,' Diana said non-commitally. 'Regardless, I would like to see Chinatown. Is it as wicked as they say?'

'I don't know who "they" are, but it's no more wicked than the Barbary Coast.'

'That is a comfort,' Diana said wryly.

As they were leaving Diana caught sight of Big Molly. Again the woman was staring jealous daggers at her. Though she pretended not to notice, Diana hoped there would be no serious friction with the big redhead who had an apparent interest in Jake Bassity.

CHAPTER SIX

The gambling den was entered through an alley off Dupont Street, Chinatown's main thoroughfare. A swarthy Chinese peered out through a slot in a sturdy door and, recognizing Bassity, admitted the couple. A second brawny Chinese conducted them through many intricate and dark passages leading up rickety stairways before finally ending in the gambling room, allaying Diana's fear that she was being delivered to Little Pete's harem that very night.

The large room was dim and hazy, with smoke from tong toys, small candlesticks supporting a bowl of peanut oil. Male and female musicians provided music to entertain the winners and console the losers. Chinese and Caucasians were betting on Fan Tan, a game played with chins (buttons or coins about the size of a penny) which the players placed in a bowl on the table and bet on numbers one, two, three or four. The croupier counted the chins off by fours with a chopstick, and the number left at the last count decided the winning number. Bassity explained to Diana that the management was fair; the croupier never touched the chins with his fingers.

'Surely there must be a way, though?' Diana asked sceptically. 'There is with every other game, no matter how "honest" the house is said to be.'

Jake Bassity grinned and nodded. 'That's what I like: a realist.'

'Well?' Diana pressed.

Bassity drew Diana away from the table, glanced about to be certain they would not be overheard, and said, 'The croupier is able to make it come out odd or even when the betting is heavy by dropping a chin from his sleeve or some other sleight-of-hand.' He took the watch from his vest pocket, checked the time, then put it away and took Diana's arm.

As she was steered toward a door leading out to a crowded balcony, Diana asked, 'I thought you came here to gamble?'

'I did,' Bassity replied easily, 'but not on Fan Tan.'

They went out on the large balcony and worked their way through the Chinese and Caucasians to the rail and stood looking down at Waverly Place. Windows and balconies on both sides of the curiously empty street were crowded with mostly Chinese. Diana was comforted by spotting Percy Wilberforce with a group of tourists and their Chinese guide on the adjoining balcony. There was a festive air of expectation and Diana turned quizzically to Bassity, who again consulted his pocket watch.

'It's almost midnight,' he announced cheerfully. 'That's when things start happening.'

Silently, men in black slouch hats, their blouses bulging with knives, hatchets and clubs, began arriving singularly and in twos and threes. 'Those are the *boo how doy*,' Bassity informed Diana, 'hatchetmen of rival tongs. It seems the *Kwong Dock* tong has a grievance against the *Po Shin She* tong, and they are going to settle it tonight. Winner takes all.'

Diana watched with misgivings while the two groups took up positions on opposite sides of the street in silence. Attending a vicious street brawl was far from her idea of entertainment, but there was no way out. 'Which tong do you have a bet on?' she asked, trying to keep her voice casual.

'The *Po Shin She.*'

Diana recognized the name of Little Pete's tong but did not let on. 'Are they the better ones?' she asked innocently.

Bassity gave a shrug. 'It depends on whose side you are on. I have some business dealings with the leader of the *Po Shin She* tong, so naturally I bet on his men.' He smiled and added, 'It's good business.'

Promptly at midnight the groups began screaming insults in Chinese. The din built in ferocity, and a few moments later a large silk cloth fluttered down from a window. It was a signal. With a flash of knives and hatchets, the men raced forward and clashed in the middle of the shadowy street. As the violent carnage raged, various onlookers cheered or groaned, according to which group they were betting on.

Wincing, Diana stood it for as long as she could, but after a man's head was split in two by a powerful hatchet blow and another's face was turned into red ruin by a two-handed slam with a club, she turned away, sickened and shuddering. She had seen men killed in gunfights but never like this. It was almost as though she had stepped back in time to the days of the Roman gladiators.

Finally a police whistle shrilled over the sounds of combat and dozens of uniformed men with drawn pistols charged up swinging night-sticks. The remaining hatchetmen scattered, leaving their dead and wounded, and vanished into the dark, dingy passages of Chinatown. The excitement over, the spectators began to disperse.

White-faced, Diana turned to Bassity and asked, 'Was there a winner?'

'The *Po Shin She*,' Bassity answered cheerfully. 'No doubt about it. They had the most men standing. I'll collect my winnings tomorrow.' He eyed her and frowned. 'Hey, you look a little green around the gills.'

Diana managed the semblance of a smile and said, 'I'm just not used to all this exciting San Francisco nightlife.' Indeed she had seen more than enough of Chinatown for one evening.

Percy Wilberforce was greatly pleased. As he had hoped, the beautiful Miss Logan was accomplishing her task and charming Jake Bassity. Tomorrow he would get a report from Sutton, at least all of the details of the evening that she chose to impart to him. Wilberforce certainly hoped Sutton was true to his word and not a jealous man. With a thousand pounds at stake, Sutton could afford to be tolerant.

The tour guide intruded upon Wilberforce's thoughts, playing the first of his two trump cards which were saved for last: a visit to an opium den where, for a monetary offering, an addict would smoke for the tourists and make an opium inspiration of remarkable length. Wilberforce smiled to himself. Unlike the gullible members of his party, he had encountered such tourist attractions in Shanghai and other exotic places and knew the supposed addict smoked no more than harmless tobacco; how else would he be ready to expound his inspirations for the successive parties of tourists that night?

Just as Wilberforce knew that the evening's finale, a 'black leper', one of the worst kind, who had been hidden from the health authorities by his countrymen for years, was merely an old man in wig, shabby clothes, theatrical make-up, and badly in need of a bath. Suggestion and poor lighting would do the rest. Still, it would be interesting to see the varied reactions of those in his party. He was sure the 'leper' would be something they could describe many times to their friends back home without losing its attention-holding value. Wilberforce dutifully fell in with his party and followed the guide from the gambling den and on to the next treat of the evening.

CHAPTER SEVEN

Far removed from Chinatown and the Barbary Coast, Jake Bassity's large two-storey house sat on a secluded lot. It was built in the gingerbread style of the day, and more than a trifle overdone, reflecting his gaudy taste. The door was opened by Li, a beefy Chinese of indeterminate age dressed in a standard butler's uniform. After sending Li to fetch a bottle of champagne from the wine cellar, Bassity proudly gave Diana a tour of the lower floor.

The parlour was very chinzy and almost feminine, again mirroring Bassity's own misplaced sense of taste. In contrast, the den was completely masculine, with dark wood panelling, a large desk, horsehair couch and chairs, and a coiled black bullwhip above a fireplace.

'That is different,' Diana remarked. 'Where I come from most men hang either a rifle or a sword over the fireplace.'

'I've had that whip since I was fifteen. I keep it to remind me of my "humble" beginnings. I ran away from home, got a job muleskinning, worked my way up, and had my own overland freight company by the time I was twenty-one. I made a killing during the war, when cargo ships were forced to sail all the way around "the Horn" to reach the Pacific Coast. After the war I made another killing by selling out before the transcontinental railroad was completed. Then I took all of my loot, came to San Francisco, and opened the biggest and best saloon and gambling house on the Barbary Coast.'

'That's very impressive,' Diana said politely. 'You certainly seem to have a knack for making money.'

'You said a mouthful,' Bassity agreed and beamed. He frowned abruptly and remarked in surprise, 'Hey, you're the first woman I ever told my life story to.'

'I'm flattered,' Diana responded, secretly doubting his sincerity.

'Anyway,' Bassity said, changing the subject, 'I was so good with a whip, I could flick a fly from a mule's ear without even touching the animal.' He saw her slightly dubious expression and nodded affirmatively. 'Bet I still could today, if I had a mule.'

They exchanged smiles, then Bassity led Diana from the room and down the long hall to a door that opened into a ballroom. A bright shaft of moonlight from a skylight bisected the large room, chairs lining two walls, and was reflected on the highly polished wooden floor.

'I don't really entertain,' Bassity said almost regretfully, 'so this room pretty much goes to waste.'

'That's a shame. A ballroom with no dancers.'

'It gets some use. There are times when I have a

lady over and Li will set up the Edison gramophone for us to dance. Do you like to dance?'

'Very much.'

'Then perhaps after we've had our champagne. . . .'

'Isn't it getting late?' Diana interjected.

'Nonsense.' Bassity took Diana's arm and escorted her to the parlour where Li waited beside a table where a tray with two glasses and an unopened bottle of champagne had been placed. They sat on a well-stuffed sofa while Li popped the cork and filled their glasses. 'This is the good, expensive stuff,' Bassity informed Diana. 'Not what's served to the customers.' They clinked glasses with a musical tinkle and drank. Bassity nodded his approval, and Li started to make a discreet exit.

It was then that the three were startled by the heavy, ornate front-door knocker pounding angrily and impatiently.

'Who the hell could that be?' Bassity exclaimed, champagne sloshing from his glass and down on his vest.

As if in answer to his question, a woman's enraged voice shrilled his name and demanded admittance.

'Big Molly,' Bassity muttered and scowled, setting down his glass and brushing at his vest.

'The redhead who did the *Mazeppa* parody?' Diana asked, already knowing and dreading the answer. From the moment she had noticed the big woman glaring at them she had sensed trouble. Big trouble.

49

'Yeah. We had a fling, and she can't accept that it's over.' The rapping and shrieking continued unabated. Bassity looked to Li. 'See if you can get rid of her.' The butler left and shut the parlour door after himself.

Uncomfortably silent, Diana and Bassity sat with eyes averted and listened to the mostly muffled voices as Li opened the front door and tried unsuccessfully to deal with the jealous woman.

'Jake,' Big Molly bellowed at the top of her lungs, 'I know you're here, dammit. And I'm not leavin' till you come to the door yourself!'

Bassity muttered a string of sulphurous oaths under his breath, then heaved a deep sigh and stood. With the expression of a man greatly put upon by the world, he said, 'I'm afraid I'll have to see her. Excuse me, Dixie, I won't be long.'

'It's Diana,' she prompted, believing he had momentarily forgotten her name in his stressful state.

'Sure it is, but I like Dixie better.' Bassity flashed a grin and went out, closing the door behind him.

Idly turning the long stem of her glass between her slim fingers, Diana waited and listened to the voices drop to an incoherent drone as Bassity succeeded in calming Big Molly's wrath. Presently the front door closed and footsteps approached. She looked up as Bassity entered full of apologies. His expression told that he'd had a very trying time and any thought of romance was gone. That was fine with her.

'If you don't mind, Dixie,' Bassity said, his

50

strained voice not quite achieving the hoped-for affability, 'I'll take you home now. Like you said, it is late.'

'Yes, it is,' Diana agreed. She set her half-empty glass on the table and rose, smiling.

'This is where you're staying?' Bassity said in mild surprise, eyeing Diana's hotel. 'It doesn't look much better at night than it does in the daytime.'

'It is clean and inexpensive,' Diana said lightly. 'And it will have to do until I find a saloon that will allow lady gamblers.'

'My offer still stands,' Bassity said hopefully. 'A hundred a week and ten per cent of your winnings.'

Diana pretended to consider, then said, 'Shall we say one hundred and fifty dollars a week and twelve and a half per cent of the winnings?'

'Done,' Bassity said and grinned. 'I can afford to be generous as long as you take in much more than you lose.'

'I never lose,' Diana said in a sultry voice, and smiled.

Matt Sutton lounged on the edge of his bed flipping cards into his new bowler hat. He'd been doing it so long he'd lost count. By now he was quite proficient, and several times the upturned hat had been moved further away to present more of a challenge. Earlier he'd been tempted to look in at the Belle La Grande, but he'd remembered Percy Wilberforce's admonition not to be seen there on Diana's first visit. True, it was a long shot that anyone would later connect the two, but there was no need in taking an unnecessary chance.

Matt missed his throw as he heard Diana enter her room. He stood and went to the adjoining door, which they both reached at the same time, both unlocking it from either side. The door opened and Diana stood smiling smugly at him.

'Guess I don't hafta ask if you got the job,' Matt drawled.

'Naturally,' Diana said simply, then beckoned him into her room. He helped her unbutton the back of her dress, and she stepped out of it, kicked off her French heels, and continued undressing. Matt slouched into the room's one chair and watched. Seeing her undress was a sight he never tired of.

Diana told of her evening, including the tong war and Big Molly's unexpected but timely appearance.

'Sounds like she's gonna be a fly in the ointment,' Matt said and frowned thoughtfully. 'I'll pass that on to Wilberforce in the morning, and maybe he'll come up with a plan to get rid of her.' He shrugged. 'Have her shanghaied or something.'

'That would be nice,' Diana said and padded naked to the dresser where she removed a long, delicate black nightgown from a drawer.

'Tomorrow I start doing my part in all this,' Matt said. 'I hope I'll be as lucky as you were, and slide right into this Little Pete's good graces.'

Diana went to the bed, drew back the covers and stretched out seductively. 'Right now,' she purred, 'why don't you come slide right into bed with me?'

'That's the best offer I've had all night.' Grinning, Matt stood and approached, unbuttoning his shirt, his mind on the pleasurable moments that lay ahead.

CHAPTER EIGHT

The next morning Boggs was lounging in the lobby reading a newspaper when Matt Sutton came down the stairs and turned in his key at the desk. Neither let on that he recognized the other. Boggs left the newspaper on a table beside his chair and ambled out after Matt. They met around the corner and Matt related Diana's news of last night.

'I'll see the colonel hears about this Big Molly,' Boggs promised. 'He's very savvy about dealing with a variety of miscreants.'

The two walked together toward Chinatown while Boggs told Matt where to find the barber shop Little Pete frequented every morning. 'It's in an alley off Waverly Place. You can't miss it. The sign is a four-legged frame painted green, with four knobs or balls on top of each leg, like the stand the barber uses to hold his washbowl.' They parted and Matt continued on to Chinatown.

An hour later found Matt Sutton loitering across the street from the alley where the barber shop was located as a stocky, rather handsome Chinese in his mid-thirties, dressed in an expensive tailored suit, long, glossy cue trailing down his back from under a derby hat, and gold, diamond-set rings and stick-pin flashing in the sunlight, strutted arrogantly along the boardwalk, followed closely by a tall, brawny Caucasian bodyguard. Judging by what Matt remembered of Percy Wilberforce's description, the man could be none other than Little Pete. He watched the two men turn into the alley and walk to the green four-legged barber shop sign. Little Pete disappeared down the stairs, leaving the bodyguard to slouch against the building and wait, something he was probably well used to doing.

Matt drew in a deep breath and exhaled, steeling himself for what he knew was inevitably coming, and started across the street, dodging the few carriages and delivery wagons as he went. The brawny bodyguard shoved himself away from the side of the building and eyed Matt suspiciously as he approached. The battered Irish face told that he liked brawling and, from his belligerent manner, he was probably pretty good at it.

'And where do you think you're going, buck-o,' the man enquired with feigned cheerfulness.

Matt rubbed his unshaved chin and replied innocently, 'To get a shave. What's it to you?'

'The barber's busy right now. You'll have to wait here or go some place else. There's plenty of other barbers about so why don't you be on your way?'

'I'm already here,' Matt said reasonably, 'and I'm sure there's a place to sit and wait down there.'

'There is,' the man agreed, and placed himself directly in front of the steps, 'but you'll hafta wait up here or else.'

'Or else what?'

'I push yer face in,' the big man said, his pleasantness vanishing, and held up a meaty fist for emphasis.

Matt kicked him swiftly in the shin. Caught by surprise the Irishman bent over and clutched at the hurt. Matt kicked his other shin. Off balance, the man teetered on the brink of the steps. Matt simply gave his shoulder a shove and the big man fell backwards and tumbled head over heels down the short flight of stairs. He came to a stop flat on his back beside the open glass door of the barber shop.

It was important that Little Pete see him administer a sound beating to the bodyguard so Matt charged down the stairs after the man, who was groaning and stirring, a hand groping inside a coat pocket. As Matt reached him, the man's hand came out of his pocket with a pair of brass knuckles. That made Matt feel better about what he had to do. Without compunction he stamped on the man's throat, not hard enough to crush his larynx but with sufficient force to keep him out of action and retching for breath a very long time. With a choked cry the big man's hands flew to his throat.

Out of the tail of his eye Matt saw Little Pete, rigid in the barber chair, and an elderly barber, hawk-billed razor raised, staring in wide-eyed surprise at the open doorway. The tong leader was well aware that he had been caught cold and was vulnerable to the stranger.

For Little Pete's benefit, Matt ended things with a brutal kick to the Irishman's groin. The brawny man spasmed, knees jerking up toward his chest, and rolled on his side with one hand still at his throat while the other pawed between his legs. Matt bent over him and hissed in his ear.

'I've a gun inside my coat. Try to come at me later and I'll kill you.'

With that Matt straightened, stepped over the man and, leaving him writhing in a ball of agony, entered the shop. He saw the flicker of fear and uncertainty in Little Pete's eyes, his face mostly lathered with soap, and the pure fear on the barber's face. 'Sorry about the ruckus, gents,' he drawled amiably and gave an apologetic smile. 'I just wanted to come and sit down while I waited for a shave, and that fella had other ideas.' He plopped down on a long bench on one side of the small room and heaved a sigh. 'That's much better.'

The Chinese remained a mute statue. Little Pete eyed Matt apprehensively. Hands trembling, the frail barber appeared ready to bolt out the door at any second.

Matt gave a casual wave. 'Go ahead on about your business. Take your time. I'm in no hurry. Got no job or place to rush to.' He leaned back against the wall, folded his arms across his chest, and crossed his legs, one ankle resting atop his other knee.

Little Pete relaxed slightly and spoke in Chinese to the barber, who composed himself with difficulty and resumed shaving him. After a moment Little

Pete addressed Matt. 'You appear to know how to end an altercation swiftly.'

'I hope you're not too put out about your man,' Matt said with feigned concern. 'He is yours, ain't he?'

'He *was*,' Little Pete said with quiet finality.

'I sorta figured that was now the case,' Matt said drily. 'Anyway, he's got a good two inches and fifty pounds on me, and I sure wasn't about to waltz with him like them prize-fighters.'

'Most prudent judgement on your part, Mister. . . ?'

'Sutton's the name. Matt Sutton. And you're. . . ?'

'Fung Ching Doy. That means Fung the perfect, but I am known by all as Little Pete.'

Matt grinned. 'Glad to make your acquaintance.'

'Now that the formalities are completed, how would you like to become my new bodyguard, Mister Sutton?'

Matt frowned thoughtfully. 'Well. . . .' he began.

'Do not be coy,' Little Pete interrupted knowingly. 'You are in need of work. That, *not* fate, brought you here.'

Matt shrugged. 'If you want to believe that, you're entitled to.' He grinned. 'Sure I'll take your job. What are you paying?'

'We shall discuss that later. You will find me most generous, *if* you do all that is required.'

'Fair enough.'

Little Pete looked to the doorway where the burly Irishman was clambering to his unsteady feet. 'You are dismissed, Dugan. Your services are no longer of value.'

'But I—' he began, speaking with difficulty.

'Do not beg,' the tong leader interrupted coldly. 'It demeans you even more. I am certain you will find suitable employment on the Barbary Coast.'

'Heathen Chi-nee,' Dugan muttered and shambled loudly up the stairs cursing to himself.

Little Pete disregarded him and looked to Matt as he asked, 'Is that how you fire most of your help?'

'When one is no longer of service. At the moment you will be most useful, until a better man presents himself.'

'Nothing lasts for ever,' Matt said philosophically.

'Sadly that is true,' Little Pete agreed. The barber finished his work and took the cloth from around Little Pete's neck and he slid from the chair. 'You have made a most judicious decision. Should you have refused my offer, you would have been killed by my hatchetmen to save face. None of my enemies can ever know that I was vulnerable for even one minute of the day or night.'

'You must have some pretty powerful enemies.'

'Every other tong in Chinatown would rejoice at my demise.'

'Speaking of demise, where are those hatchetmen of yours? I only saw Dugan outside.'

Little Pete snapped a command in Chinese. A door at the back of the shop opened and a man stepped out, pistol in hand. 'There are two others discreetly hidden in the alley.'

'You are cautious, aren't you?' Matt drawled and unfolded his arms, revealing he held the six-gun from inside his coat.

Little Pete nodded and smiled approvingly. 'I trust you will be similarly cautious with my life.'

Matt grinned and returned the pistol to its shoulder holster with a twirl. 'You'll be just as safe as in your mother's arms.'

CHAPTER NINE

It was early evening but things were already in full swing along the Barbary Coast when Diana Logan arrived hurriedly at the Belle La Grande. She was ushered through the employees' rear entrance by a burly, middle-aged bouncer who took her to one of the dressing rooms and then left. There were six chairs before mirrors on a long make-up table in the brightly lighted room. Five had women's articles strewn about, so she put her reticule in the empty place, then removed her cape and hung it quickly with the other capes and dresses on a clothes rack. Afraid of being late, she had changed into her brief black gambling outfit in her hotel room and slipped a cape over it, before rushing out for a hansom cab.

Diana had seated herself at the table and was touching up her make-up when the hall door banged open abruptly and Big Molly, in her Mazeppa costume, came storming into the dressing room. The door rebounded off the wall and slammed shut again, with an equal loudness. 'Hey, you blonde piece of fluff,' she shrilled. 'I been looking for you!' She stalked straight to Diana, who did not turn as she smoothed powder over her cheeks with a small brush.

'It is considered good manners to knock before entering,' Diana said, with a calmness she did not feel, and eyed the woman's reflection in the mirror.

'Aw, stow that "little Miss Southern belle" tripe, dearie,' the big woman said hotly, standing pressed against the back of Diana's chair. 'It also ain't considered "good manners" to try and steal another gal's fella!'

Diana kept her eyes on their mirrored images and continued her work, even though her make-up was already impeccable. 'I am *not* trying to steal any one from any one.'

'Says you!' The redhead glowered down menacingly at Diana's reflection. 'You're quitting your job tonight. There's plenty of other saloons around to work at.'

Diana set down the brush and inspected her appearance in the mirror. 'I already have a job here,' she said simply, 'and I need the money very badly. I am staying for the time being, so there is nothing more to discuss. Now, if you will kindly excuse me, it is time for me to deal cards.' She made to rise but never completed the movement.

Surprisingly swift for a big woman, Molly wrenched Diana's arms behind the chair, and, holding her slim wrists crushingly in one hand, snatched a black fishnet stocking draped over the back of the next chair. She wound it deftly in and out and around Diana's wrists, then yanked the ends together and knotted them so viciously the coarse mesh sank deeply into her flesh. The small, tight ball was high up between Diana's wrists, well out of reach of her fingers.

Tingling fingertips starting to numb, Diana gasped in anguish and regained her shocked senses. She had badly miscalculated the extent of the woman's jealousy. She opened her mouth in protest, but Molly pulled a dagger from her mass of upswept red hair and put its tip under her chin, forcing her blonde head back to look directly up at her.

'Now that I got your complete attention,' she hissed, her overly made-up face a frightening mass of pure hatred, 'listen to me good, missy.' Ever so slowly she let the blade trace the contour of Diana's face lightly with its sharp tip. Diana sat silent and rigid, not daring to move a muscle. 'I've had trouble with you hoity-toity ones before, but they're all gone, and I'm still here. And it'll be the same with you.' Her large green eyes became narrow slits as they bored into Diana's terror-wide blue ones. 'I ain't real heartless, so you got three days to find another job. If you're still here after that, I'm gonna carve up this pretty face so bad no man will be able to look at it without getting sick to his stomach.'

Long nails digging into her palms as her hands balled into tight fists, Diana strove to retain her composure. As with most truly beautiful women, she appreciated her good fortune and enjoyed the admiration of others. The threat of being horribly mutilated sent an icy fear coursing the entire length of her body.

They were abruptly aware of clicking French heels and women's chattering voices approaching along the hall, and Molly tucked the dagger back into her thick hair. 'Remember what I said,' she cautioned. 'And if you're smart you won't tell Jake about this!' She eyed Diana hard for emphasis, then turned as the door opened. Three gaudily dressed and made-up dancehall girls entered and halted inside the room at the unexpected sight that greeted them.

'Say, what's going on?' a henna-haired woman demanded.

'I'm just saying "hello and goodbye" to the new girl,' Molly answered casually. 'She's leaving by the end of the week.'

The second woman, attractive in a cheap way, strode forward ahead of the others, pointing. 'Hey, what the hell did you do to my new stocking, Molly?' she cried and, brushing past the big woman, stopped behind Diana and picked at her tied wrists. 'It ain't supposed to be used like this. And the knot's so damn tight it'll have to be cut.'

'Tough,' Molly said with a shrug and walked away.

The woman stopped her work and called, 'You owe me for a pair of stockings.'

'I don't owe you nothing,' Molly said without looking around, 'but a bust in your fat mouth if you don't shut the hell up.' The other two women quickly cleared a wide path as she strolled from the room, leaving the door open.

'Bloody cow. . . .' the second woman muttered in frustration and looked to the others. 'Can either of you undo this?'

Diana craned her slender neck and looked up at the woman. 'I am sorry about—' she began.

'It's not your fault, honey,' the woman interrupted sympathetically. 'That big bitch bullies all of us girls, damn her.'

The two women joined them, and the henna-haired one gave the knot a try. 'Don't never tangle with Big Molly,' she cautioned as she plucked futilely at the twisted mesh ball. 'Her favourite thing in a fight is to grab a girl and fall to the floor on top of her. Then she punches her and bounces up and down on her till she's out like a candle.' She heaved a heavy sigh and stepped back, defeated. 'I'm about to break a nail. You try it, Claudia.'

The third woman nodded and took a turn at the impregnable knot. 'And she's real good with a knife too,' she said. 'She keeps one hidden in her hair, and she can whip it out in the blink of an eye.'

'We've seen her slice up more than one girl,' the second woman said solemnly.

Diana nodded. 'She showed me her knife just before you came in.'

'Molly is also good at knot tying,' Claudia said, stepping back and shaking her head.

Diana glanced about imploringly at the three and asked, 'Couldn't you please find someone who can cut this? My hands are cold and numb. If I'm not untied soon, I may not be able to deal tonight.'

Before anyone could reply, there were hurried high heel footsteps, and a woman called cheerfully, 'Tony is here, girls. Grab your purses.'

65

'Tony will free you,' the henna-haired woman said confidently.

Diana stared confusedly at their brightly smiling faces and asked, 'Who is he?'

'Why Tony Gamble is the king of the hoodlums,' the second woman answered. Then she added, 'You really are new here, aren't you?'

Diana remembered what Percy Wilberforce had told her and Matt about the hoodlums. 'Do you pay him for protection?' she asked, frowning.

'Heavens, no,' Claudia said and laughed. 'Every week he has naked pictures taken, then goes through the saloons and red-light district selling them for fifty cents apiece.'

'Isn't that rather expensive?' Diana remarked, aware that the average worker's pay was only a dollar a day.

'They are worth every penny,' the henna-haired woman said dreamily. 'He has a wonderful body, and he shows just everything!' She tittered like a mischievous child.

A plump, dark-haired young woman rushed into the room eagerly and, more intent on finding her purse, spared the group a cursory glance. 'He's right behind me,' she announced breathlessly and pawed through her things.

Diana was left sitting miserably while the three women scrambled for their purses or reticules. She tensed as a man's footsteps came jauntily along the hall and a deep, uncultured voice called charmingly: 'Here comes Tony, girls, ready or not.'

Diana turned her head toward the open doorway.

The thought of sitting there helpless in front of the so-called king of the hoodlums was a bit disconcerting, but she felt that he surely wouldn't try to take advantage of her situation with the other women in the room. She was about to find out. The footsteps were almost outside the doorway.

CHAPTER TEN

Straining to see through the fog shrouding a lonely beach some miles south of the city, five armed men of the *Hep Sun* tong waited patiently for a signal from a ship off the coast. When it came with a break in the fog, a lantern was lighted hastily and the signal was returned.

The men waited and cast cautious glances about the beach for the authorities or a rival tong, unaware that their guard on the cliff above had been disposed of silently, as well as the driver of their wagon, marked 'vegetables' in English and Chinese, by six of Little Pete's hatchetmen.

Matt Sutton had been sent along merely to observe, unless the men ran into something they could not handle and needed a fast gun. He hoped that would not be necessary, as he had nothing against the rival tong and figured whatever the dispute, it was strictly a Chinese affair.

The ocean was dark, whenever it could be glimpsed through the blanket of fog. Finally a light, much closer than before, flashed briefly. It was evidently from a boat that was checking its course. The lantern on the beach confirmed its direction, and then served as a beacon, flashing on and off at intervals for the next twenty minutes. Slowly a crowded longboat emerged from the thick mist. It was pulled up on to the beach, and its occupants were urged to hastily disembark.

From his vantage point above, Matt counted a dozen small Chinese, in blue peasant coats, trousers and slippers, their heads wrapped in large handkerchiefs. He had expected the contraband to be bales and boxes of silks and other expensive articles from China, not people. The men were being smuggled past Immigration officials, but what did Little Pete want with them? Were they craftsmen with valuables in the bundles each carried? Perhaps some had wealthy relatives here or in China who would pay their ransom?

The boat put back out to sea and vanished quickly in the fog and blackness. Lantern glowing eerily through the wisps of fog, the silent procession wound its way up a narrow path. It wasn't until they gained the top that Matt was able to learn the real reason Little Pete wanted the new arrivals. They were women: slave girls.

Matt wanted no part of it. The rival tongs could fight for possession of the women and kill each other off for all he cared. He only hoped no one had informed the authorities about the landing, as he had no wish to trade shots with the Law. Still, he was on probation with Little Pete and it was important to gain his complete confidence.

The women were hustled into the closed wagon, and it was then that the bodies of the driver and guard were found nearby. A man started to raise an alarm but a hurled hatchet split his face in two. Brandishing knives and hatchets, Little Pete's men charged from the swirling fog. Colt out and ready, Matt stood by in case he was needed. He hoped that wouldn't happen, as a gunshot would be heard for miles and might draw unwanted attention to their presence.

The battle was brief and vicious. Like ghastly spectres, the two groups surged in and out of the obscuring mist that made the sounds of combat all the more unsettling. When it was over, all of the *Hep Sun* hatchetmen lay dead and the women in the wagon were in the hands of the victors.

There followed a betting contest on distance as the bloody bodies were hurled unceremoniously to the beach below, where the tide would later wash them out to sea. Those not devoured by sharks and such would be deposited like human driftwood somewhere far down the coast.

Then Matt and his group headed back to San Francisco to turn the frightened women over to Little Pete for sale at an auction, which very coincidentally was to take place at midnight.

Percy Wilberforce and a group of wealthy guests from his hotel were taking an arranged tour of San Francisco nightlife that naturally included the Barbary Coast. As one of a party of 'swells', he would be able to ascertain how Diana Logan was faring her first night on the job at the Belle La Grande without drawing overt attention to himself. Also, he wished to observe her competitor with the colourful name of 'Big Molly'. Then he would decide how best to remove her from the scene with the least amount of fuss and bother, so that Miss Logan would be unhindered in gaining and maintaining Jake Bassity's favour. That in itself should be a simple task for the young beauty, and for the necessary amount of time required until Countess Arabella Stanton was rescued, Jake Bassity would consider himself a very lucky man.

Wilberforce almost wished he were slim again and twenty years younger. Then he remembered the follies and foibles of youth and decided he was better off as he was.

CHAPTER ELEVEN

'Good evening, pretty ladies, one and all.'

Dark leather satchel slung over one shoulder, Tony Gamble, king of the hoodlums, stood posed in the doorway, an arm raised in a casual greeting and a wide grin on his face. Extraordinarily handsome in a coarse fashion, he was tall, wiry, with dark, wavy hair, and in his mid-twenties. His tight black suit emphasized his physique, and Diana suspected that it had been carefully calculated to do so. It was easy to see why he was so popular with the Barbary Coast ladies.

Squealing like happy schoolgirls, the women crowded around anxiously as he moved to the table, set the satchel down, then opened it and removed three photographs. 'Here they are, ladies,' he said personably. 'Fifty cents each, or all three for only a buck-fifty.' He set them out, then noticed Diana just sitting there and eyed her with avid interest. Her tautly drawn-back shoulders hitched up her firm breasts and caused them to almost spill over the low top of her scanty outfit. 'Don't be shy, beautiful.

Come have a free peek. You might see something you like.' He grinned widely. Diana smiled and shrugged.

Not taking her eyes from the photographs, the second woman said, 'Big Molly has been up to her old tricks. She tied the new girl in that chair with *my* stocking.'

'We'll fix that,' Tony said charmingly and left the women ogling his pictures. 'I'm always ready to oblige a lady in distress.' He stopped behind Diana and inspected the imprisoning knot. 'She did a real good job, didn't she?' He took a folded knife from his coat pocket, shook it, and a large blade sprang from its handle. 'Now don't move.' Diana had no intention of doing so. Breath tight in her chest, she sat frozen while, with a careful yet seemingly casual flick of his wrist, Tony severed the stocking. 'Sorry, Gertie,' he said to the second woman as he stepped back and put the folded knife away. 'There was nothing else to do.'

Already resigned to the loss of her stocking, Gertie said, still eyeing the pictures, 'That's all right, Tony, I forgive you.'

Diana gave a deep sigh of relief as the stocking unravelled from her aching wrists like a black snake. 'Thank you very much,' she said to Tony and, wincing, brought her arms in front and let her numb hands fall limply into her lap.

'Don't mention it,' Tony said. He smiled charmingly, then excused himself and returned to his customers.

Diana chafed her wrists gingerly and grimaced at

the fiery pinpricks dancing over her skin as her circulation sluggishly returned. She was so absorbed in her own distress and thoughts of how she would deal with Big Molly within three days' time, that she didn't notice Tony come up with his satchel after finishing his transactions with the women.

'You ready to feast your eyes on my manliness?' he asked, and flashed a wide, toothy grin.

'Perhaps later,' Diana answered evasively. 'I'm already late. I was supposed to be out front dealing faro over fifteen minutes ago,' she smiled and held up her red-marked wrists, 'but, as you saw, I got tied up.'

Tony considered, then gave a broad shrug. 'I've got some time to kill. I'll go with you and see that no one else ties you up.'

For the next hour Tony hung around the faro table as Diana's self-appointed protector. All but serious players were quickly discouraged from loitering and trying to get overly friendly with the beautiful new dealer. Diana's game was a bit off, thanks to a gnawing concern over Big Molly. The woman was not bluffing, yet Diana had to cultivate Jake Bassity. Something definitely had to be done to remove the dangerous threat of the jealous woman.

Diana was relieved when the announcement came that the 'big show' was about to begin, and there would be no gambling until it was over. She and Tony took a small table in front of the stage. Saying she needed steady hands, Diana declined his offer of a whiskey and, to the waiter's disapproval (as all the girls were expected to order an expensive drink that was actually weak tea, which she hated), asked for a sarsaparilla. While they waited, Tony proudly showed her his belt made of 'Chinaman's' pigtails, and Diana smiled politely. Then he displayed his arsenal that he was never without: brass knuckles, a hickory bludgeon, the large knife he'd used to free her, and a slingshot and lead pellets.

'This would certainly give someone a terrible headache,' Diana commented, fingering a heavy pellet.

'You bet,' Tony agreed and grinned.

'I used to have one as a child,' Diana said and picked up the slingshot. 'I was pretty good, too. Though I never shot birds, animals, or people.'

'You missed all the fun.'

Their drinks arrived. Diana ignored the waiter's scowl as he served her root beer in a tall, frosty beer mug. Tony paid and the man left. Diana cutely fired the empty slingshot at his back. The show started, and to divert her mind from the awful acts, which the audience seemed to enjoy, Diana continued to fret about Molly. By the time the big redhead came on stage as Mazeppa, Diana had her answer.

Borrowing a pellet for the slingshot, she let fly while Tony watched with an anxious grin. It had been a while since she had used one, and her aim was off. She hit the donkey. The result was just as satisfying. The braying, bucking beast fell over the footlights carrying Big Molly with it and almost annihilated the orchestra, bringing gleeful hoots and howls from the audience. Swearing like a sailor, Big Molly crawled from under the thrashing donkey and, seeing Diana laughing and still holding the slingshot, rushed forward with murder in her eye.

Molly yanked Diana up, held her tightly and fell to the floor on top of her. Having been forewarned, Diana was expecting the move and managed to wriggle free. Then, to the crowd's further delight (as a cat-fight was much more entertaining than two men slugging it out, particularly when one of the combatants was a slender, statuesque, scantily dressed blonde beauty), the women rolled about scratching, slugging, kicking, and hair-pulling. Adrenalin and desperation combined to turn Diana into a wildcat, and the bigger woman realizd quickly that she had an unexpected battle on her hands, one she might very well lose.

Hurling Diana back against her table's leg and nearly upsetting it, Big Molly sat up on her knees and, reaching up into her wildly dishevelled hair, whipped out the partly protruding dagger. 'Damn you to hell, bitch,' she shrieked, spewing spittle with her words. 'I'm gonna cut you up every which way.'

Glancing about urgently, Diana spotted her heavy mug. She shoved herself to her knees, snatched it, and hurled the contents into Molly's face as the big redhead lunged at her with the blade.

Momentarily blinded by the sticky root beer suds, Molly screamed in rage and sat back on her haunches, pawing at her face with her free hand. Well aware that the woman truly meant to disfigure or even kill her, Diana walloped Molly across the side of her head with the mug just as hard as she could. Giving an agonized cry, the big woman crashed to the floor and the blade leapt from her hand and clattered away.

With the crowd's eager urgings, Diana straddled the big redhead as she tried to crawl to her dagger and, aware that she must hurt Molly so badly she would never dare to retaliate, began flailing away on her head with the thick glass mug. Only when Molly was completely unconscious were two burly bouncers able to drag Diana, fighting and kicking, from the badly bleeding woman, amid the crowd's cheers.

Jake Bassity shoved through the mob, gathered what had happened in a single, sweeping glance, then smiled at the sight of the previously aloof, immaculate blonde, hair and clothes in extreme disarray, still lost in her rage as she thrashed madly in the men's grip, blood-dripping mug clutched in one slim hand. 'Awright, folks, the show's over,' he said cheerfully. 'The gambling tables are open again. Everybody drink up and have a good time.'

The bouncers released Diana, who was beginning to simmer down, before Tony Gamble could push his way through the slowly dispersing crowd and intervene on her behalf. She looked down at the bloody mug as though seeing it for the first time, then shuddered delicately and dropped it to the floor.

'A little late for squeamishness, isn't it, Dixie?'

Bassity remarked, amused. Still attempting to regain her self-control, Diana made no reply. He looked to the bouncers. 'Mack, fetch an ambulance for Big Molly.' The man nodded and rushed off. 'Murphy, do what you can for her till it comes.' The other man looked dispassionately at the unconscious woman, then grabbed a bar towel from a passing waiter's arm and knelt to wrap her head in it. Bassity waved Tony away. 'Go have a drink on the house, Gamble. The tigress here and I have some business to discuss.' Begrudgingly, Tony headed toward the bar. Bassity spared a glance at the redhead, who was ignored by all but the morbidly curious. 'So Big Molly finally met somebody she couldn't shove around,' he mused, then looked to Diana. 'And even a proper lady has a touch of the fishwife in her.'

Composed, Diana smiled and said flippantly, 'Now you know about women.'

Bassity grinned, then motioned, 'Let's go to my table.'

Diana brushed her tousled hair back from her face. 'I must look a mess.'

'Everybody's already seen you,' Bassity said as they weaved through a maze of tables and people. 'Besides, mussed or otherwise, the customers think you're great.' As he seated her at his table, the distant clanging bell of a hospital wagon grew steadily louder. 'Thanks to you I need a new Mazeppa.' He sat across from her. 'And you're elected. I'd say that's only fair.' He braced for an argument.

Diana could scarcely believe her good fortune. The way to gaining Bassity's good graces was open, now that the obstacle of Big Molly had been removed, and she planned to take full advantage. She pretended to consider, then gave a casual shrug. 'Fine . . . but *no* donkey. I play Mazeppa bareback on a horse, as it's supposed to be.'

'Agreed.'

Diana cocked her head and recalled her idle thoughts the previous night when, in boredom, she had speculated about how she would play the part. 'I'll do it differently . . . still in pink tights, but sitting up sidesaddle with my hair down over my shoulders in front.'

Bassity grinned at the mental image and the effect it would have on his customers. He should pack the place every night. Then he remembered and, frowning questioningly, asked, 'But Mazeppa is supposed to be tied on the horse?'

'Of course,' Diana agreed and pressed on with feigned enthusiasm. 'Only my hands will be tied behind me, and there will be a band around the horse's middle with a ring to hold on to. It will also anchor the ends of a length of filmy cloth arranged discreetly over my lap.' She paused deliberately to let Bassity again summon up her image, then continued. 'A runway could be extended out into the audience, then collapsed and put away after every performance.'

'You're pretty ambitious with my money.'

'We both know I will draw a bigger crowd.' Diana motioned to Big Molly's sprawled form as the ambulance drew to a halt in front and its loud bell stopped. 'Who did the people cheer for during the fight?' she asked knowingly.

Bassity nodded in agreement. The crowd had chosen a new favourite and had no further interest in their old one. He and Diana watched two white uniformed attendants bustle in with a canvas stretcher and go to Big Molly, who once more became the centre of attention for a macabre moment. Briskly, they lifted her on to it, then carried her off.

'I'd say that's the last we'll see of Big Molly,' Bassity commented almost wistfully. 'You did such a thorough job that I doubt she will ever show her face on the Barbary Coast again.'

Diana sincerely hoped he was right. She was surprised to notice Percy Wilberforce sitting at a table with a party of swells and beaming as Big Molly and the attendants disappeared out the batwing doors. Presently, the ambulance pulled away with its bell clanging loudly. Inwardly Diana heaved a sigh of great relief, then continued planning her act with Bassity.

For a moment Diana's thoughts were engaged in amused speculation about Matt's reaction to her becoming the new 'Flame of the Barbary Coast'. Then a splash drew her attention to a swamper with a pail of soapy water mopping up Big Molly's blood, and she was sobered by the realization that it might well have been her own, and she had narrowly escaped being the occupant of the hospital wagon. There was no time for foolishness. She and Matt were playing a dangerous game that would end in death if they became careless. Resolved, she forced her mind back to the business at hand.

CHAPTER TWELVE

The *Hip Ye Tung* tong controlled the slave traffic and maintained a sales room, known as the Queen's Room, in the basement of an unpretentious building on Dupont Street, and it was there that Matt and his group delivered the women to Little Pete. Since only wealthy Chinese (mostly tong members) were allowed at the auctions, Matt waited outside while Little Pete went in surrounded by his hatchetmen. Again, Matt was to be ready to use his six-gun should the enraged shouts of the *Hep Sun* tong escalate into combat with Little Pete and his men.

The auction was delayed for a time as insults and threats were hurled and both tongs came to the edge of violence. Fortunately, the cooler heads of the *Hip Ye Tung* prevailed (mainly for selfish monetary reasons) and it was agreed that an accounting would be kept on every sale. Whenever the expected mandarin from Hong Kong arrived, he would rule on the matter as well as try to effect a peace between Little Pete and the various tongs he had outraged.

Hours later, Little Pete strutted out with his

entourage and the profits from the sales, minus the
Hip Ye Tung's commission. Matt accompanied Little
Pete to his lodgings and was then dismissed until
noon.

Tired and despondent, Matt arrived at his hotel.
He knocked lightly on the adjoining door, got no
response, and decided that Diana must be sleeping
soundly. She probably had an equally wearing
evening, and he had nothing to say that couldn't
keep till morning.

'Go away . . . I am not receiving . . .' Diana called
sleepily in answer to Matt's less timid morning
knock.

'It's almost eleven,' Matt called through the door.
'I'm leaving for work shortly.'

There was a pause, then a heavy sigh, followed by
bare feet padding slowly to the door. A key turned
in the lock, and Diana, face mostly hidden by her
long, dishevelled blonde hair, opened the door in
the black diaphanous nightgown.

'Good morning,' Matt said cheerfully and
hugged her to him.

Diana gasped and drew back. 'Don't touch,' she
said, wincing. 'I've had a very bruising night.'

'Sorry,' Matt said, releasing her. He watched as
she stumbled back to the rumpled bed and threw
herself down gracelessly across it on her stomach.
Matt went over and sat beside her on the edge of
the bed. 'I'll tell you about my night,' he said, trying
to keep the concern from his voice, 'if you'll tell me
about yours.'

Speaking sleepily from under her cascading hair, Diana told of her adventurous night and assured Matt that she was perfectly able to take care of herself, and with the exception of some aching muscles and a few bruises, she was otherwise undamaged.

In response to her *Mazeppa* act, Matt only shrugged. 'Let 'em look all they want,' he said casually, 'but I'm the fella you come home to every night.' Then he went on to relate the events of his night, and when he'd finished it was time to leave for work.

After a long goodbye kiss, Matt was careful to return to his room and go out his own door into the hall, in case unseen eyes were watching either of their rooms, and Diana roused herself reluctantly to start her day.

Outside, Matt found a hansom cab waiting with Percy Wilberforce inside. 'Do join me, Sutton,' he said jovially. 'It may be a tight fit, but we'll manage.' Matt gave the driver Little Pete's address and settled in beside the fat man with a bit of room to spare. 'How is your lady faring this morning?' Wilberforce asked as the cab pulled away.

'She's none the worse for wear.'

'You really should have been there, old son. I have seen women's altercations before, but nothing to equal last night's.' Wilberforce gave a deep, throaty laugh. 'The way Miss Logan ingeniously disposed of Big Molly by belabouring her head with a beer mug was most admirable. It saved us the delay of plotting how to be rid of the woman without being obvious.'

Matt wished that he had been there. It was a different and unseen side of Diana, whom he'd always considered gentle and ladylike. He knew she had a temper when put upon, and there had been occasions when he'd been the recipient of both her verbal and silent wrath (which was much more disconcerting than the former), but he'd never seen her in a physical confrontation.

Wilberforce dug a derringer from an outside coat pocket. 'From now on, it might be best if Miss Logan kept this with her,' he said and handed the small weapon to Matt. 'It fits easily into her reticule or, forgive the indelicacy, under her skirt and against her thigh.'

'Thanks,' Matt said and dropped the derringer into a coat pocket. 'I'm sure Diana will appreciate this.' He then gave a terse report of both his, and the rest of Diana's night.

'It's a pity Little Pete did not decide to keep at least one of the slave girls for his harem,' Wilberforce said. 'If we had that location, this venture might well have been concluded success-fully this very day.' He gave a broad shrug and said in resignation, 'Well, at least, that appears to confirm his preference for Caucasian women.' Then he added hopefully, 'There is still time for you to find the harem. And I dare say that Miss Logan will make a most splendid Mazeppa, which could lead Little Pete to induce Jake Bassity to turn her over to him shortly after her first appearance.'

'From what Diana says, Bassity has his own plans for her.'

'So much the better. Friction between the two will work in our favour most advantageously. It would give the greatest satisfaction to play them against each other.' He beamed at the thought. 'There are no more bitter enemies than when thieves fall out.'

Matt saw they were nearing Little Pete's building and said, 'I'd better get out here and walk the rest of the way.'

'A most judicious decision,' Wilberforce commented and rapped the roof above them with the brass head of his walking stick for the driver to stop.

Matt climbed out and began walking while the cab turned off and headed along another street. It might be too much to ask for, he thought, but he hoped to locate Little Pete's harem today. If not, then at least before Diana could become his latest trophy.

Little Pete was dressed and waiting when a servant showed Matt into his living quarters. The stories about the tong leader never wearing the same suit twice seemed correct, as the shiny blue silk suit was different from the others Matt had seen during the brief time he'd been employed.

'I am pleased you are punctual, Sutton,' Little Pete said cheerfully. He picked up a large satchel from a table. 'Today we take weekly collections from storekeepers.'

Matt shrugged and said easily, 'Whatever you want.'

'I want,' Little Pete said and handed the empty satchel to Matt.

*

For the next few hours Matt and Little Pete walked the streets of Chinatown that were his tong's designated territory, going in and out of shops along the way, where protection money was handed over with feigned politeness. Any tale of hardship fell on deaf ears. Little Pete would look the picture of true sorrow and ask the shopkeeper to commiserate with him about the 'most high' cost of maintaining 'adequate' protection for his 'most esteemed friends' from such dangers as fire or vandals. Deep concern for the safety of his friends *and* their families quite often kept him awake nights. Understanding the not-too-subtle hints the reluctant storekeeper would then wisely pay his cash tribute for the week.

The satchel was bulging by the time Matt and Little Pete finished their rounds and walked back to the tong leader's building. After locking the money away in a large floor safe in a corner of his bedroom, Little Pete had his carriage brought around and announced they were going to the race track.

'The race isn't until Saturday afternoon,' Matt said.

'True,' Little Pete replied. 'But I must ensure the winner ahead of time.' He gave a toothy grin. 'That way, make plenty money.'

They drove to the race track, and Matt was given a thick packet of bills before they stepped from the carriage. They wandered about the stables, appear-

87

ing to be studying the horses and watching them train, and Matt caught sight of Percy Wilberforce and several affluent-looking men also seemingly studying the horses and jockeys.

Behind a stable, they met Billy Tobin, the jockey of Saturday's favoured horse, who through bribes and intimidations had agreed to throw the race. Matt handed over the money to Tobin, thus supposedly keeping Little Pete's hands clean should anyone happen to witness the pay-off. Business completed, Matt and Little Pete returned leisurely to his carriage and left.

Back in Chinatown, Matt was dismissed for the night. Little Pete was staying in to go through his financial bookkeeping and also hold meetings with several of his hatchetmen. Trouble was again brewing with rival tongs, and the mandarin, an influential, high-ranking official from Hong Kong, might be arriving sooner than expected. Little Pete considered his tong American, and therefore beyond any rulings from officials from Old China.

Matt still did not know the location of Little Pete's harem, but there was always hope for tomorrow. He returned to his hotel. Diana was working, so he flopped down on his bed and tried to forget the events of the day.

Sure, he was just doing a job that would sooner or later lead to the rescue of a kidnapped noblewoman. Mercenary reasons aside, it was something he should be proud of accomplishing. But in the meantime, stealing slave girls, intimidating frail, little old shopkeepers, and even a jockey, did not instil pride in oneself.

Again reassuring himself that it was all a means to an end, Matt closed his eyes and made his mind a blank. In almost no time he was asleep.

CHAPTER THIRTEEN

For the next two weeks Diana worked with a white horse and its trainer, Duffy, a short, middle-aged Irishman who had been with a circus until he found that a more lucrative living could be made on the Barbary Coast. A great believer in the old saying 'God invented whiskey to keep the Irish down', Duffy imbibed but was never drunk during practice, for which Diana was thankful. Whether it was out of respect for her or fear of Jake Bassity she was unsure. Still, there was a slight trepidation on her part the first time her hands were actually tied behind her back for the ride. Duffy remained a perfect little gentleman, even when Diana began wearing the flesh-coloured leotard that would be in the act.

Since Jake Bassity was footing the bill, he insisted that Diana make a nightly appearance at the Belle La Grande for several hours and deal faro. What with work, *Mazeppa* rehearsals, and an occasional late night supper with Bassity, Diana's full schedule hardly left her any time for Matt. Because of her pending star status and being the owner's new girl, she was given the private dressing room that had previously belonged to Big Molly, even though she was not yet a performer. Tony Gamble still hung around her faro table and flirted, much to Jake Bassity's chagrin but he could not risk provoking the king of the hoodlums, for fear of not only a boycott but also a rowdy, destructive incursion of the street toughs into the saloon.

Diana noticed a change in her fellow workers. Even the few women who had been friendly now seemed distant, as though by association they might somehow displease her and she would have them fired. With the exception of Emma Landry, the terrible singer, who was off in her own little world (wearing a cardboard coronet with bits of coloured glass and telling all that she was the illegitimate daughter of an English earl), the performers kept their jealousies just below the surface and were coolly polite. Diana was there to do a job and not win popularity contests with the help. Still, it was a bit disconcerting to be a social pariah.

During the times she could not beg off having late night suppers with Jake Bassity or dancing in his ballroom to a gramophone set up by Li, she managed to keep him at bay, but it was becoming progressively harder to do. She wished Matt or Percy Wilberforce would hurry and find where Lady Stanton was being held. That ranch she and Matt talked about owning was becoming more appealing with each passing day – and night. Keeping that goal in mind, she continued to play her part.

Then one night things almost came to a head. Bassity had taken her home in his carriage and insisted on seeing her up to her room. Diana delayed purposely in unlocking her door and said goodnight, giving him a peck on the lips.

'C'mon, Dixie,' Bassity said, slipping his arms about her slim waist and holding her tightly against him, 'you can do better than that.'

'Please, Jake, I'm very tired,' Diana said wearily and gave a wan smile as she pushed gently against his chest with both hands.

'What you need—' he began, retaining his hold on her squirming body.

'What I need is rest,' Diana interrupted firmly. 'Working late in the saloon, and then getting up early to rehearse with the horse becomes awfully tiring after a while.'

'You can have tomorrow off,' Bassity said and crushed his mouth against hers in a harsh, demanding kiss. Diana emitted a muffled gasp as her soft lips were mashed painfully against her teeth. Bassity slowly broke the kiss as Diana kept her lips carefully unresponding. 'Now let's go inside and . . .' He broke off as heavy footsteps mounted the stairs. Inwardly relieved, Diana used the distraction to slide her key into the door lock.

Matt Sutton reached the top of the stairs, saw Diana and Bassity standing very close together and paused, fighting back the impulse to seize the saloon owner by the back of his collar and the seat of his pants and give him the 'bum's rush', as the bouncers called it, down the stairs and eject him out into the street.

'What the hell are you gawking at?' Bassity growled, irritated by the intrusion.

'Didn't expect to see anybody in the hall this late,' Matt replied with forced nonchalance.

'Awright, now skedaddle!'

'You folks are blocking my door.'

Diana unlocked her door and quickly stepped partway inside. 'Suppose we let the man by, Jake,' she said sweetly, then flashed a devastating smile. 'I'll see you tomorrow.'

The mood broken, Bassity nodded glumly and watched her close the door. He heard the key click the lock into place and turned to reluctantly take his leave. The tall man, who looked slightly out of place in a suit, vest and derby bowler, stood watching him. Bassity was tempted to take his frustration out on him but caution said that would not be wise. Though the man looked and sounded like a hayseed, there was a strange coldness in his eyes that forewarned of danger.

Drawing himself to his full height and puffing out his chest, Bassity swaggered toward the stairs. Matt walked forward in an easy manner and gave a polite nod as he passed. The saloon owner nodded back and kept walking. He noticed that the stranger was taller and more muscular, and was secretly glad that he had obeyed wisdom and not goaded him into an exchange of words that might have ended in fisticuffs and the real possibility of coming out second best. He hesitated at the top of the stairs and cast a glance back curiously, to see the stranger unlock his door and disappear into his room, which was indeed next to Diana Logan's room. Satisfied that the man had been telling the truth, Bassity descended the stairs.

The interruption had put Bassity in a foul mood and he decided that tomorrow he would again push for Diana to move into a more respectable hotel. Jealousy briefly had its way with him and he wondered if her previous refusals to change hotels had anything to do with her rather handsome next-door neighbour, as, judging by his accent, they were from the same region.

By the time Bassity climbed into his carriage he had logically dismissed his previous thoughts. There were many Southerners in San Francisco and outlying areas. Most had left the war-devastated South in search of a new life, and the man was probably no different. Though the Reconstruction had ended, the South was still recovering from the ravages of not only the war but the carpetbaggers. His mind eased, Bassity slouched back in the seat and directed his thoughts to business.

Slipping off his coat and vest, Matt relaxed and gave Bassity time to depart the hotel before knocking on Diana's door. She answered it quickly, barefooted and in a wrapper, and ushered him inside.

'Thank heavens you came back when you did,' Diana said, then gave a weary sigh and leaned against his chest. Matt's arms encircled her, holding her close. 'Jake is becoming even more persistent, and I have yet to learn a thing.' She leaned back in his arms and looked up at him. 'How about you?'

Matt shrugged. 'Nothing. But sooner of later Little Pete is bound to start longing for some female companionship.' He flashed a grin. 'Just like me.'

'Oh?' Diana said, feigning coyness, and arched a slim eyebrow. Her eyes held his for a long moment. Slowly a sultry smile spread over her face. 'A woman can have a similar longing . . . for the "right" man.'

Matt lowered his face to hers and their lips met in a tender kiss that grew into passion.

CHAPTER FOURTEEN

It was several days later that Matt accompanied Little Pete to a large wholesale shoe factory on the edge of Chinatown. While the workers were Chinese, the salesmen were Caucasian, to prevent customers who might be prejudiced against Chinese from knowing who made the shoes and that F.C. Peters and Company was in actuality Little Pete. Matt was left to wander about the two lower floors of the factory and inspect the variety of shoes on display in the sales room and go up to the second floor and see how they were made, while Little Pete disappeared into one of the upper levels of the sprawling four-storey building to go over the company's books.

A cowboy, Matt had little interest in city shoes, much less how they were made, and soon became bored waiting. He noticed two hatchetmen slouched by the stairs leading up to the third floor, and guessed other men were stationed on the remaining floors. He reckoned they were to guard the money in a safe somewhere upstairs. Since neither man spoke much English, Matt could not learn a thing.

At closing time the Caucasian salesmen and the Chinese factory workers left by separate doors, and Matt was alone with the hatchetmen, still waiting restlessly for Little Pete. A few minutes later things started happening.

There were slight sounds in the stock room. The two hatchetmen at the foot of the stairs dismissed them as a rat. Out of boredom Matt went to investigate, anyway.

It was a rat, all right. A human one, with a sharp knife and hatchet for teeth. He saw Matt and drew back both weapons to throw.

Matt's draw was lightning fast. Not chancing that the man might be wearing chain mail beneath his blue tunic, he shot him in the face.

The bloody head bobbed violently on its shoulders and the man slammed against a rack of shoe boxes, then wilted to the floor amid a shower of boxes and men's shoes.

Smoking pistol ready, Matt eased further into the room and surprised a second thin hatchetman squeezing through a small, black-painted window that had been jemmied open. He also shot him in the head and left the body blocking the window. No sooner had the deafening gunshot faded than Matt heard sounds of violence out by the staircase. Gun in hand, he charged from the room.

The two guards were sprawled in pools of their own blood at the foot of the stairs, along with an intruder. Matt saw eight men with knives, hatchets and pistols racing up to the second floor. He reached the stairs in time to shoot the last man in the back of the head and bring him flopping back down, leaking brains and gore as he came. Matt leaped over the body as it slammed to a halt against the others, and then took the steps in two and threes to the next level.

He reached the second floor, where the guards had also been killed. An intruder was splay-legged on the floor, holding his belly and staring in dumb wonder as his slimy grey intestines slithered from a gaping red slash from hip to hip. A wounded or dying man can kill you just as dead as a healthy one, so Matt dispassionately shot him in the head, ensuring that he did not try for the pistol and hatchet on either side of him.

Sounds of fighting and dying echoed from the third floor but Matt delayed to shove more shells into his pistol, as he might well need more than the two bullets remaining in its chambers.

Bolting up to the third storey, Matt arrived to find the next two guards leaking their life's blood all over the floor while now five intruders battled on the stairs with the two guards from the fourth and final floor. Taking a man with them, the guards went down under a flurry of knives and hatchets.

Matt's chilling Comanche war-cry halted the four startled intruders in their tracks as they were about to rush up the stairs. Once heard the hair-raising cry was never forgotten, and it still unsettled the nerves of many a brave frontiersman who had heard it before.

The Chinese whirled, wide-eyed and terrified, to see that it was merely a mortal man behind them and not some sort of demon. Before they could regain their senses and use their weapons, Matt held back the trigger of his six-gun and fanned the hammer, spraying them with hot, deadly lead. Blood geysering in profusion, the four did grotesque jigs, one man's pistol aborting into the steps and kicking up a shower of splinters in all directions, then collapsed like rag dolls as Matt's Navy Colt clicked empty. Almost in unison the men tumbled down to join the other dead men in forming a human barricade about the foot of the stairs.

A funereal quiet slowly settled over the large factory room and Matt realized that he was the only man alive and standing. Even so, he hastily reloaded his six-gun. The spent shell casings sounded unnaturally loud as they clattered over the floor.

Keeping the gun in hand, Matt waited a long moment, then finally called: 'Hey, Pete, the fight's over. We won. You can come out now.'

At first there was no reply. Matt was uncertain whether to go up there or let the tong leader come to him. Could be Little Pete was up there with ledgers and stacks of money spread all around an open safe, and he might feel it was a very tempting sight to Matt, who'd just take a notion to shoot him dead, make off with the money, and blame it on the rival hatchetmen. Then the decision was made for him.

'I shall be with you directly, Sutton,' Little Pete called. Hurried footsteps moved across the floor above. Clothes dishevelled, Little Pete came down the stairs. That was strange, as none of the attackers had succeeded in reaching the fourth floor. He jumped nimbly over the tangled bodies at the foot of the stairs, then asked, 'Where are the rest of my men?'

'I'm it,' Matt replied. He pointed to the rival hatchetmen. 'There was ten of 'em, as far as I saw. You'd best get yourself a better class of fighting men. I ain't bragging, but if I hadn't been here right now you'd be saying "howdy" to all your honourable ancestors in the Happy Hunting Ground or whatever you folks call it.'

'I am greatly in your debt, Sutton.' Little Pete led the way down the stairs, noting the carnage on every level. 'There are men from several tongs. I did not expect them to band together so quickly and then act.'

'You been rubbing them raw for some time.'

'Yes, but it was last night that I refused Leong Lum Fung's attempt to discuss a peace treaty with the other tongs.'

'Who is he?'

'The mandarin who has arrived from Hong Kong to try and effect a settlement with the San Francisco tongs. I will not be dictated to by an outsider.'

'I don't rightly blame you.'

'The fool told me that my doom was sealed, and he would remain in America, if only to attend my funeral, which was not far off.' Little Pete laughed derisively. 'He will grow even older waiting.'

They left by a side entrance and wound through a maze of dingy alleys. On reaching the safety of his lodgings, Little Pete sent word for the shoe factory to be cleaned up before it opened for business the next morning. With the promise of a bonus for his actions, Matt was given the night off and told not to report for work until the following evening, as Little Pete would be busy until then holding a war council and seeing that reprisals were carried out against the various tongs.

'You figure it's healthy going somewheres at night?' Matt asked, hiding his disappointment. Diana was opening her *Mazeppa* act, and he'd been looking forward to seeing it.

'I cannot hide here like a frightened rabbit. I must present a bold face for all my enemies to see.'

'If you say so.'

'Tomorrow evening should present a most intriguing diversion. There is a new act opening at the Belle La Grande, where I am a silent partner with the owner, Jake Bassity.'

'You seem to have your finger in all sorts of pies,' Matt said casually, not letting on that he was well aware of the tong leader's involvement in the acknowledged biggest and best saloon on the Barbary Coast.

Little Pete nodded and continued. 'Mister Bassity assures me that not only is the woman quite good but she is also quite beautiful. We shall judge for ourselves, eh?'

Matt was secretly pleased by the news, but it

presented a problem. 'How in blazes am I going to protect you in a saloon full of people?'

'Do not concern yourself. I have a private box sheltered from prying eyes. You shall see. Now excuse me until seven o'clock tomorrow night. I have much to do.'

Matt left and walked toward his hotel with a lot on his mind. A tong war had started and that could complicate things. He might be too busy protecting Little Pete's life to tend to the business of locating Countess Arabella. And if Little Pete was to suddenly wind up dead, how would the harem ever be found?

Matt was almost to the hotel when he suddenly remembered Little Pete's rumpled appearance at the shoe factory. A fella doesn't get that way from just going over the books and counting money. Could be he'd taken off his chain-mail vest to be more comfortable while he was working, and then put it back on hastily while the fighting was going on below him . . . Then again, suppose he'd just come from his harem? The top floor of the shoe factory would be as good a place as any for it.

Matt walked on, mulling it over in his mind again and again. By the time he reached his hotel he'd decided that he was going to have a look up on that fourth floor the first chance he got. How and when he'd accomplish that, he did not know but he was determined to do so and have his answer one way or another.

CHAPTER FIFTEEN

Opening night for the highly touted new *Mazeppa* act had finally come and the Belle La Grande was packed with a loud and lively crowd, from Nob Hill society to the toughest Barbary Coast riff-raff that ever robbed a sluice or stoned a Chinaman. All waited impatiently for the big event.

Little Pete and Matt Sutton were admitted through a side door that led into one of the rooms of Jake Bassity's office. The saloon owner gave Matt a cursory glance but was preoccupied with business matters and did not appear to recognize Little Pete's latest hireling. Matt waited out in the hall while the two partners conferred. Presently Little Pete joined him and they went up a flight of stairs to the second level where the private boxes were located.

Nearest the stage, the box had curtains on each side and the four chairs were set back from the rail, so Matt and Little Pete sat in darkness. A curving runway extended from the stage, and the two would have an excellent view when Diana passed on her horse. Though Diana had assured him that the animal was well trained, Matt hoped it would not be spooked by the huge, rowdy mob.

Diana secretly shared Matt's concern as she peered out from a small peephole in the over-decorated curtain. Suddenly she wished she hadn't. She had been fine during the many dress rehearsals in the morning hours before the saloon opened for business, with only the swampers and other employees watching, but now it was before a real audience.

Not being a professional actress, Diana was overcome with a case of butterflies in her stomach. She had heard stories that even the most hardy, experienced thespian still experienced stage fright before a performance, and it was a perfectly natural occurrence. That was fine and dandy for others, but outside of the thought that 'misery loves company' it did nothing to cheer her. There was far too much at stake for her to let her bravado slip and make a fool of herself. Also, her pride would not settle for an unintentional parody. The audience might not mind, but she was *not* Big Molly.

'Is the crowd as big as it sounds?' asked Pearl, a tall, big-boned, coarsely attractive woman. She and three others were hold-overs from Big Molly's act.

'See for yourself,' Diana said, her voice not as steady as she wished, and stepped aside with a rustle of her stage cape.

Pearl took a look and exclaimed in awe, 'Mercy me, we never ever had this many for Big Molly, or anybody else that I can recollect.' She turned and saw Diana's face was pale despite her make-up. 'There ain't nothing to worry about, dear,' she said cheerfully. 'You'll be just swell, and they'll all love you. Just you wait and see.'

Diana managed a smile and thanked her. She was the last act so there was time to compose herself as best she could. She wondered if Matt and Little Pete had arrived and, if so, which box was theirs?

The crowd was in no mood for encores from the preceding acts and any attempt was met with boos and catcalls. All had been tolerated begrudgingly and the audience's patience was now at an end. *Mazeppa* was finally announced and there was a thunderous ovation. The announcer was scarcely heard above the slowly dying din as he dramatically set the scene. With no apology to Lord Byron (not that many in the audience were familiar with his epic poem to begin with), Mazeppa had been changed to a young Amazon queen whose evil half-sister usurped her throne and ordered her banished, tied naked on a horse, out on the endless Steppes.

The racket began all over again when the curtain rose to reveal Diana, in a long, diaphanous cape, standing between two women in brief Amazonian costumes while Pearl, the evil half-sister, stood smirking. Amid the mandatory boos and hisses directed at a villain, Pearl emoted her lines of banishment with a melodramatic intensity worthy of any member of a third-rate touring company. Then came a deafening cheer when Diana recited her one line of brave defiance with an equal zeal.

At Pearl's angry command the two women removed Diana's cape with a flourish, and there was a collective gasp as her magnificent, statuesque body, arms tied behind her at the wrists and elbows, appeared naked under the stage lights in a flesh-coloured leotard. Her blonde hair flowed down over her sharply drawn back shoulders and partly hid her boldly thrusting breasts. The group froze in a tableau, with Diana posed courageously and giving the audience an ample eyeful.

In their box, Little Pete, eyes fastened solely on Diana, remarked to Matt, 'Bassity was correct. Is she not indeed most exquisite?'

'Sure,' Matt agreed, surprised that he too was as caught up in the scene as the audience. Though he had often seen Diana naked, this simulation was every bit as alluring and again made him realize how lucky he was to have such a beautiful woman in love with him. Jealousy briefly had its way with him at the thought of Diana in Jake Bassity's arms, much less being forced into Little Pete's harem of white women. Then his thoughts returned to the play as the tableau again came to life.

Pearl called for the horse and the audience waited in silent anticipation. A fourth Amazon led the white horse on stage and an eager murmur went through the crowd. While Pearl gloated villainously the three women boosted Diana carefully atop the horse in a side-saddle position, then arranged her cape modestly about her lap and affixed it in place to hide the large ring in the band around the horse's middle that she gripped with her tied hands.

A lusty cheer went up as Diana and the horse were sent on their way. Pearl and the three women disappeared quickly offstage as the horse pranced and trotted out on the runway and passed slowly before the audience.

Out of the corner of his eye Matt saw Little Pete lean forward in his chair for a closer look at Diana as the horse went by then turned back on to the stage. He knew Diana was an excellent horse-woman, but he hoped the boisterous crowd would not turn her mount into a real runaway.

For over five minutes the horse went up, down, and back and forth on the stage and out along the runway repeatedly, before Duffy finally called to it from one side of the stage. To the audience's disap-pointment the horse obeyed and carried Diana off into the wings. There was a moment's silence, then wild applause.

'See, what did I tell you?' Pearl said cheerfully and led the horse and Diana back on stage. The trained horse took a bow with Diana still seated tied, then Pearl led the animal slowly back into the wings.

In their box, Little Pete looked over the audience and nodded approvingly. 'Bassity has made a most wise choice, has he not?'

'Yeah,' Matt agreed, trying not to show much

enthusiasm. Secretly he was proud of Diana.

'We will remain a while longer,' Little Pete announced. 'I must consult with Bassity about the woman. Now that she has proven herself.' He smiled. 'There is indeed much profit to be made before the public tires of her.'

'That looks like it might be a long time.'

'I hope so. Either way I have plans for her.'

CHAPTER SIXTEEN

To Diana's surprise the first visitor to her dressing room was Emma Landry. And even more surprising, her gushing praise seemed to be very sincere. This was the first time Diana had been alone with the bird-like woman and, noting her cardboard coronet, she decided to play a hunch.

'I heard that an English earl and his wife actually came to the Belle La Grande last year. Was he any relation to you, Emma?'

'Oh, I remember,' Emma said, her face glowing. 'They came with only a guide instead of with a party of swells, like so many of the rich ones do. The earl was no relation, but he was ever so nice. Real democratic.'

Jake Bassity had intended to be waiting in Diana Logan's dressing room when she finished her act. Unfortunately business with Little Pete had detained him. Both had agreed the girl was a gold mine that should be worked until the vein petered out. With proper publicity that might not be for a year, maybe more. The prospect put him in an even better mood. As long as the act was bringing in money there was no danger of Little Pete demanding Diana Logan for his harem of white women. Bassity enjoyed her company, and when that time came (there was no doubt that the tong leader was taken with the tall, blonde beauty) it would depend on how their relationship was faring, as to whether or not he defied Little Pete. That would be far down the road so there was no sense dwelling upon it until the time finally came.

Bassity had taken a good look at Little Pete's new bodyguard after the show and had recognized him as the man in the hotel room next to Diana Logan. It was probably a coincidence that could be dismissed by the old saying: 'It's a small world.' Still, it was strange that the tong leader's bodyguard and the Belle La Grande's latest attraction were both Southerners and lived right next door to each other.

As he neared Diana's dressing room, Bassity put aside all thoughts but celebrating tonight's triumph. He walked up and raised a hand to knock but hesitated at the sound of women's voices. He identified them as those of Diana Logan and Emma Landry, and out of idle curiosity, he eavesdropped for a moment. What he heard brought a dark scowl and seemed to confirm the suspicion that had been lurking in the back of his mind. Diana was slyly questioning crack-brained Emma about the English earl and his wife, who was now the prize ornament in Little Pete's harem. The more he heard, the more convinced he became that the questions were not merely innocent inquisitiveness on her part. Diana Logan was a spy in the pay of the Earl of Stanton or one of his agents.

Restraining the urge to burst in and angrily accuse her, Bassity turned and strode away. He would later make an excuse for not coming to her dressing room, but at the moment his rage and disillusionment were too great for him to act convincingly as though nothing were wrong. It burned his pride to be taken in like a drunken miner at one of his own gaming tables. He needed to confer with Little Pete, and without his new bodyguard being around. It was one meeting Bassity certainly was not looking forward to, as in Little Pete's eyes he had 'lost face'. He had given the spy a job, built her up to the public, and after tonight's performance there would be a hue and cry if she were to suddenly disappear or meet with a tragic end.

Bitterly damning fate, Diana Logan, and anyone else he could think of, Bassity stomped into his office, where he poured a stiff drink then sat behind the desk and gloomily composed himself before sending word to Little Pete to meet him privately at his house late that night.

The meeting took place at 3 a.m. in Bassity's study. Little Pete listened patiently to Bassity's tale and then remarked sternly, 'I am most distressed by this, Mister Bassity. You have invited a serpent into our midst.'

'If you hadn't gotten ideas above your station and grabbed that earl's wife, instead of staying with Barbary Coast girls, none of this would be happening,' Bassity shot back defensively.

'What is done is done,' Little Pete said calmly. 'Now we must deal with the woman discreetly, and not too hastily.'

'Agreed,' Bassity said, then took mean pleasure in adding, 'While we're at it, you may have "invited a serpent" into your own midst.'

'How so?'

'That new bodyguard of yours has a room next to the Logan girl, and they're from the same Southern state.'

'That proves nothing.'

'They both started work at the same time too.'

Little Pete was gravely thoughtful for a long moment. Then he reached a decision and gave a heavy oral sigh. 'I shall regret to lose Sutton, but capable bodyguards abound in San Francisco. Innocent or not, he must be sacrificed. We cannot do otherwise. The risk is too great.'

'Want it to be a killing, or look like an accident?'

'Neither.'

'But you just agreed to get rid of him!'

'Sutton saved my life.'

'I'll handle it and you can keep your hands clean.'

'No. Sutton shall take an ocean voyage. My debt will be paid and I will have saved my honour.'

'Maybe so, but he could come back later and make trouble.'

'That will not be for a very long time. And if so, you may then deal with him.'

Bassity gave a shrug of dismissal and said, 'It's your funeral.'

'I think not,' Little Pete said unperturbed.

'What about the girl?'

'They should both disappear at the same time, so that neither will be suspicious of the other's disappearance and inform their employer.'

'Fine.'

'Naturally, the young lady shall become the newest addition to my "House of Women",' Little Pete said and smiled in anticipation.

'But first I want some time with her,' Bassity said harshly. 'I don't like being played for a fool.'

'I understand,' Little Pete agreed, then eyed Bassity evenly and cautioned, 'She is not to be marred or damaged too badly, so that I cannot enjoy her company while she recovers from what you have done to her.'

'Yeah, sure,' Bassity muttered. 'You'll get your "Yellow Rose of Texas" with her petals drooping but intact. Now when will all this happen?'

'Soon, but we must await a propitious moment. Until then we must earn as much profit from the girl as possible, as recompense for what we shall lose when she disappears.'

Bassity nodded. 'I'll increase her performances, then when she does disappear everybody will be told she's exhausted and taking a rest. I'll find a new girl to spell her, and pretty soon folks will forget about her.'

'There are times your wisdom leaves me in awe,' Little Pete said drily. Seeing Bassity's perplexity at the double-handed compliment, he smiled and raised his whiskey glass in a toast. Bassity gave an uncertain smile, raised his glass, and they drank.

CHAPTER SEVENTEEN

A week passed, a hectic one for Diana Logan who had abandoned her faro table in order to do as many as six performances of *Mazeppa* a night, from late afternoon to early morning. She would return to her hotel room, collapse into bed exhausted, and sleep most of the day away, seeing very little of Matt Sutton. At work she would chat briefly with Emma Landry, but she could learn nothing more about the Earl of Stanton and his wife than she had during their first conversation.

Boggs and Percy Wilberforce made occasional separate appearances at the Belle La Grande, subtly keeping a protective eye on Diana since Matt was occupied even more than he'd been previously with Little Pete's nefarious business dealings. Tony Gamble often came to her dressing room, particularly whenever he was making the rounds with his satchel of naked pictures of himself.

Curiously enough, Jake Bassity seemed less attentive than usual. Though it could be dismissed as simply being too busy with the nightly overflowing crowds and understanding the strain of her fatiguing schedule, Diana could not help but wonder if he had grown tired of their non-sexual romance.

Wrapper over her pink leotard, Diana was resting on her dressing-room sofa after the late afternoon performance and gently rubbing her rope-marked wrists. Occasionally one of the women would tie her tighter than necessary, either inadvertently or out of secret jealousy. Since the ropes had to be secure and not hang loosely or fall off, she was resigned to the slow-fading marks for the run of *Mazeppa*. Being tied up was not new, even on a running horse, for she and Matt had encountered more than their fair share of bad men during their long and difficult trek to California. At least this time there was no danger involved and she was being well paid for the discomfort.

A knock on the door interrupted Diana's thoughts and Jake Bassity entered, all smiles and charm. 'Guess what, Dixie?' he announced cheerfully.

'The saloon is burning down and I don't have to perform tonight?' Diana had always hated guessing games and was annoyed when people tried to be cute and did not just come right out and say whatever they had to say to begin with.

'Close, but not that drastic.'

Diana sighed her exasperation and sat up, swinging her long, lovely legs over the side of the sofa and feeling with her toes for her French-heeled slippers.

'You have planned extra performances.' She smiled sourly, then added, 'But you will make it up to me by finally allowing me a day off tomorrow.'

'I'm doing even better than that,' Bassity said affably. 'After your next performance I'm giving you the rest of the night off, and you're coming to my house for a big surprise.'

'Surprise?' Diana repeated, puzzled. She had never been one for surprises; often they had been something she could have done without.

'You'll love it, you'll see,' Bassity assured her. 'I won't keep you too late, and tomorrow you can honestly have the whole day and night off. How's that?'

'Wonderful.' She frowned thoughtfully and asked, 'Jake, are you sure you want to do this tonight? Saturday always has a big crowd.'

'I can afford it,' Bassity said, his manner apparently open and frank. 'Besides, you've gotta have a night or two off sometimes, and that mob better start getting used to it.'

'I won't argue,' Diana said and smiled her delight.

'My carriage will be waiting for you after the next show. I'm going on ahead to tend to some business and then prepare things for you.'

'I should go to my hotel and change.'

'No need to. It isn't formal. Just you and me, so wear what you already have.'

'My saloon dress?'

'Sure.'

'All right,' Diana said and shrugged indulgently.

Bassity grinned. 'Don't worry, you look good in anything.' With that he went out.

Diana sat mulling over the curious turn of events. As much as she longed for some time off, why had Jake Bassity chosen tonight, and also given no previous inkling of his plan? Could he somehow have learned her true reason for working there? It did not seem possible, but there was no telling.

Then a much more pleasant thought came to her. Perhaps Bassity planned to reward her with an expensive gift, such as an engagement ring? That would present a thorny dilemma. To refuse could lead to her dismissal. To accept would mean that he expected a much closer relationship from tonight on.

Telling herself not to worry needlessly ahead of time, Diana rose and went to the dressing table, where she began touching up her make-up for her last performance of the night. How she wished it were her final performance, ever!

CHAPTER EIGHTEEN

Something was wrong.

For the past week Matt Sutton had sensed that he was being watched. The question was by whom? He and danger were old adversaries, and he had long ago learned not to ignore the familiar cold, empty feeling in the pit of his stomach that came whenever things were not right.

Were Little Pete's enemies planning to cash in on the reward posted for his death, or was the danger from the tong leader himself? Matt had no idea how Little Pete would have uncovered him as a spy, as he was very careful about the few meetings with either Boggs or Percy Wilberforce, but he could not rule out that possibility. Though nothing had been said, Jake Bassity might have recognized him as the man with the room next to his star attraction. Still, unless Diana were under suspicion (which to her knowledge she wasn't), there was no reason for Bassity or Little Pete to think anything about it.

Matt had wanted to somehow find out what exactly was on the fourth floor of the shoe factory but there had been no chance to do so. As he walked back towards his hotel he was tempted to make a detour in that direction, until he became aware of light footfalls behind him in the shadows. Listening tensely, he walked on and tried to discern if there were two sets of footsteps.

There was no doubt that he was being followed. No attempt was made to pass him, even when he slowed his stride. He was still unsure if more than one man trailed him along the dark, empty street.

Reaching a corner, Matt cut across hurriedly to the opposite side of the street as a carriage went past and ducked into a doorway. Sure enough a Chinese started across after him. He did not have the appearance of a hatchetman but looks were often deceiving. Matt lunged out from the doorway and blocked his path as the man came up.

'All right, what are you doing following me?' Matt demanded roughly.

The man froze, his face mirroring apparent surprise, and shook his head innocently, as though he did not understand English.

'Don't give me that "no sabe" rot,' Matt snarled and reached a hand out for the man's tunic.

The movement was never completed. A short club sailed out of the darkness behind him and slammed against the back of Matt's head. A second before unconsciousness took him Matt had the realization that there was indeed a second man.

Diana Logan had finished her last performance of the evening and was changing in her dressing room for her engagement with Jake Bassity when there was a knock. Looking toward the door over the top of her dressing screen, she called, 'Come in,' and hoped no change in plans had occurred. She was relieved when Tony Gamble entered with his satchel.

'Good evening, lovely lady,' the king of the hoodlums said charmingly. 'I've sold all of my latest pictures, so how about joining me for some supper between shows?'

'I'm sorry, Tony, I'm through for the night. Jake's carriage is waiting.'

'Let it wait.'

'I can't. Jake is expecting me. He has a surprise for me at his house.'

'It might be nothing,' Tony said and slacked into a chair.

'He is my employer.'

'Yeah, sure. And he's been working you as hard as that horse you ride.' He eyed her in confusion as she stepped out from behind the screen in her brief saloon-girl dress. 'I thought you were changing?'

'I have. Jake said this would be fine.'

'Looks fine to me,' Tony agreed, giving her the glad eye. 'Still, it don't seem quite right for this so-called "special occasion" of sorts.'

Diana gave an unconcerned shrug and gathered her reticule and street cape. Secretly she shared Tony Gamble's suspicion and had tucked her derringer against a thigh, held there by a red garter. The evening might be no more than Jake attempting to seduce her with an expensive pretty, but she could not afford to take chances. That was the trouble with spying, even things that turned out to be innocent were first suspect.

Reluctantly, Tony Gamble stood and trailed Diana from her dressing room to the employees' rear entrance. 'I'll be around here a while,' he said as they stepped outside, 'in case you make it an early evening with old Jake.' He grinned and patted a coat pocket. 'All this money is just itching to burn a hole in my pocket, and I don't mean to spend it on gambling.'

'I can't promise,' Diana said evasively, 'so don't wait too long on my account.' All she wanted to do after leaving Jake Bassity's house was go to her room, luxuriate in bed, and sleep until morning, even longer if she could. She favoured Gamble with a sweet, parting smile and went to the waiting carriage.

Tony Gamble started to turn away and go back inside when he heard Diana comment to the driver holding the door open for her that he was not the regular man. Curious, he delayed and listened.

'No, missy,' the Oriental in driver's livery replied politely. 'He sick. I am Li's brother, Lem Jung. He ask me be Mister Bassity's driver this night.'

Gamble stood watching as Diana entered the carriage and the driver closed the door after her then climbed up on the box and, with a shake of his whip, started off along the alley. Maybe it was because he wasn't all that fond of Jake Bassity, but Tony Gamble had a feeling that he was up to something. Hell, he had nothing better to do, so he decided to follow the carriage and hang around outside Bassity's house (which he'd never seen before, anyway) in the event he was right and Diana Logan needed a protector.

Tony sprinted to the street and went in search of a horse to appropriate from one of the hitching rails. A few minutes later he was in discreet pursuit of Diana's carriage as it plodded along in the heavy Saturday-night horse, foot, and carriage traffic entering and leaving the Barbary Coast district.

Matt Sutton groaned himself awake.

For a time he wished he hadn't done so. It was quiet and cosy in the oblivion of darkness, and his head did not ache. He was afraid to open his eyes, for fear he would see his brains laying about for folks to step on. Hesitantly, he raised a hand to the back of his head and very gingerly explored the throbbing lump of flesh that felt as big as a goose egg. His touch was agonizing and sent messages of pain screaming to his brain. At least his scalp wasn't bleeding and his skull wasn't broken, so he let his hand flop back down on his chest.

Having been knocked unconscious frankly more times than he cared to remember, Matt was familiar with the queasiness that invariably came upon awakening. The rocking motion of his surroundings and the overpowering stench of polluted sea water didn't help his stomach any, nor did the constant creaking of wood and tackle help his pounding headache. He slowly opened his eyes and, after his blurred vision cleared, saw that he was in a dim room. Coils of thick rope were strewn beside several boxes and a pattern of moonlit squares from above illuminated the area about him. He was sprawled against the side of a short flight of stairs leading up to the deck of a ship. Matt had never been aboard a ship before, and under other circumstances he might have found it enjoyable. The realization of what had happened sliced through the grogginess shrouding his brain and brought complete alertness.

He had been *shanghaied.*

As though in confirmation a gruff voice from above shouted, 'Cribbins, see that our new crewman for Valparaiso is comfortable until we sail.'

'Aye, Cap'n,' answered an equally rough-toned voice, and heavy footsteps stomped across the deck.

Matt's head protested the sudden movement as desperation goaded him clumsily to his feet. A sweeping glance showed there was no weapon of any sort. The footsteps halted and the hatch cover with its ventilation squares was removed. Matt ducked urgently behind the stairs as the man started down, belaying pin clutched warily in one hand. When the man's feet were in reach Matt seized an ankle and yanked with what force he could muster.

With a startled cry the brawny sailor somersaulted the remaining steps and crashed face down in a wide spread-eagle. Matt lunged out from his hiding place and kicked the man in the side of the head while he groped groggily for his dropped club. The man went limp. Matt scooped up the belaying pin and, head still sending signals of displeasure to his brain, stole up toward the open hatch.

Three sailors were in various parts of the moonlit deck, none looking in his direction. Matt bolted up and made for the gunwale. Before he could scramble atop it and leap over, a strong hand grabbed his shoulder and spun him around – right into a meaty fist. The brutal impact sent him sprawling backwards across the top of the gunwale.

Still gripping the belaying pin, Matt struck out blindly as the thickset sailor who had materialized from the shadows caught him by the throat, holding him in place, and drew back his fist for another blow. Simultaneously there was an ear-splitting howl of utter anguish and the sickening crunch of bone and cartilage. Nose and cheekbone smashed, the bloodied sailor sank to his knees, dragging Matt with him to the deck. Matt put his shoulder behind another wallop, this time to the base of the man's skull. The choking hand fell away and the man slumped in an unconscious heap.

Shouts of discovery brought Matt staggering to his feet. A uniformed ship's officer and two sailors came charging across the deck. Matt hurled the short club at the officer, who was in the lead. It caught the officer in the centre of his forehead with a solid *thonk* and dropped him to the deck in the path of his men who went down in a mad tangle of arms and legs.

More sailors were rushing on deck and the enraged captain was gesturing down at him and directing them from the raised poop deck while vowing horrible retribution in between sulphurous oaths. Matt knew damn well that he'd best get off the ship pronto, for there was no doubt a watery grave awaited him before the voyage was over. Hoisting himself up on the gunwale, he pinched his nose and dropped over the side into the dark, waiting sea.

The cold salt water stung his bruises and shocked Matt into even greater alertness. He broke the surface, shivering and gasping for air, and saw the docks a hundred or so yards ahead. Behind him pandemonium reigned aboard the ship he had just quitted. He gulped several deep lungfuls of air and dove back beneath the water before he could be spotted and a boat lowered.

Matt swam for all he was worth through the murky water in the direction of the docks until his empty, near-bursting lungs forced him to frantically stroke and kick his way up to the surface. Treading water, he looked about him. The docks were less than thirty yards ahead. He threw a glance back and saw a longboat with several men, one holding a lantern, being lowered over the ship's side. Matt turned away and ducked beneath the water once more.

When Matt bobbed to the top again he was beside one of the docks' timber pilings. Several rowboats were tied to a landing with stairs that led up to the street. He swam over and pulled himself out of the water then collapsed, muscles trembling uncontrollably like a freshly landed fish, striving to catch his breath.

Out in the harbour voices shouted back and forth from the ship and the circling longboat, its high-held lantern casting its bright light searching about over the inky water.

Matt drew himself up into a crouch and made his way quietly to the stairs. Keeping a heedful eye on the distant longboat, he went up to the street. No one was lurking about. Staying to the shadows, he hastily took his leave of the waterfront.

CHAPTER NINETEEN

The carriage drew to a halt in front of Jake Bassity's dark, silent house. The driver leapt down, opened a door and helped Diana out. She went to the front door, which opened abruptly before she could seize the heavy brass knocker, and Li ushered her inside. Diana entered, unaware that Tony Gamble sat a horse and watched intently from the shadows thirty yards away. She heard the carriage start away as the door closed behind her, then followed Li to the ballroom, where he informed her that Bassity would join her presently, then closed and locked the door. Diana's senses heightened with the sound of the key turning in the lock and she glanced about nervously.

The centre of the large room was illuminated by the bright rays of a full moon shining through the skylight. Breath tight in her chest, Diana wondered if Bassity had somehow found out about her. Pulling her cape tightly about her, she began moving toward the darkness. Her high heels and the rustle of her short skirt were magnified by the silence. She froze abruptly in mid-step at the sound of the key turning in the lock, then whirled toward the door as it opened and blinked as a pillar of light from the hall brightly invaded the room.

His elongated shadow falling over her, Jake Bassity stood framed in the doorway in his shirt-sleeves, a long bullwhip dangling menacingly from one hand. 'Hello, Dixie,' he said without warmth and stepped into the room, pulling the door shut behind him and again reducing the room to only pale moonlight. 'We've some important business to discuss in private.' He locked the door from the inside and put the key in a vest pocket while Diana watched wide-eyed and tried to find her voice. 'I don't like being made a fool,' he said, slowly moving toward her. 'Now who are you and this Sutton working for, Pinkerton or some other detective agency?'

'I don't know what you are talking about.' Diana said with feigned innocence, letting more of the South come into her voice.

'I was hoping you'd be stubborn,' Bassity said. He halted a short distance from her and popped the whip in the air. Diana flinched as the whip cracked like a gunshot in the large room. 'You might as well talk. Your partner has been shanghaied and is on his way to Chile. That's in South America, not the Mexican food,' he added and laughed.

'I still don't understand,' Diana said, attempting to keep her voice even. 'But if you hurt me I'll say anything you wish, whether it's true or not.'

'I do intend to hurt you before you are turned over to Little Pete's harem, where you'll spend the rest of your youth, until you lose your looks.' He drew back the whip. 'Tell the truth, and the beating won't be as bad as it could be.'

Fighting back her rising panic, Diana hurled her reticule at Bassity as a diversion, then her right hand dove under her skirt for the derringer against her black-stockinged thigh.

A snap of the whip burst Diana's flying reticule and showered its contents widely about the room.

Haste and fear conspired against Diana and her fumbling fingers almost dropped the little gun as she wrenched it from the garter, then out from the hem of her short skirt.

'A gun,' Bassity cried in mock fear. 'We can't have that!'

Before Diana's unsteady hand could take aim the whip seared the back of her hand, leaving an angry red weal. She shrieked at the burning agony and the gun leapt from her hand, hit the floor with a bounce, then went skidding away. Clutching her smarting hand, Diana stared nervously after the retreating gun. Then she whipped off her cape, sailed it at Bassity, and started to bolt for the derringer.

The whip batted aside the cape easily, then flicked out and encircled one of Diana's slim ankles, yanking her off her feet. She hit the unyielding wooden floor hard and, with a strong rush of air, the wind was driven from her willowy body.

Eyes and face alive with sadistic fury, Bassity advanced slowly, his rapidly flailing arm sending the whip whistling and cracking. Diana screamed and reared as the whip stingingly sliced the back of her dress to ribbons. She scrambled across the floor, then huddled in a protective ball as the whip popped above and around her tauntingly and resumed rending her dress into pieces.

The actual blows to her flesh were light stings, but she knew all too well that Bassity was only playing with her for the moment, as a cat would a mouse. Stripped to a torn black chemise, fishnet stockings with red garters, and high heels, she shoved her protesting body up to her knees.

The long whip snaked around Diana's waist and forearms, pinning them to her sides. Laughing, Bassity advanced, keeping tension on the whip. His feet tangled in her cape and an object beneath it from her reticule shifted under his foot, causing him to lose his balance. With a cry of surprise, he smashed down painfully on one knee. Feeling the whip's taut grip slacken, Diana wrenched her arms free, grabbed it in both hands and yanked frantically as hard as she could.

Bassity was flung forward and slammed face down on the hard wood floor, his nose breaking with an appalling snap. Overcome with excruciating pain, he watched through tearing eyes as his victim threw the whip off into the darkness, then stood and went in search of the gun. Disregarding his anguish, Bassity shoved himself up and, bellowing his rage, charged after Diana.

Heart and lungs pounding wildly, Diana heard Bassity's ominous footfalls and quickened her pace as much as she dared in her high spindly heels on the polished floor. She was nearing the derringer when Bassity made a long, desperate leap. Sliding on his stomach, he reached the gun and scooped it up before she could. Bassity rolled on to a hip and sat up, cocking the hammer as he raised the small gun. Diana was on top of him and lashed out with a foot.

Bassity jerked his hand aside to keep Diana from knocking the derringer from it and her high heel sank into his right eye and penetrated his brain. The shot was explosive in the quiet room as the gun discharged, its slug whining waspishly past Diana's ear, and shattered the skylight's glass which rained shards down on the two. Bassity fell back, his free hand ripping the shoe from Diana's foot, clutching the derringer tightly in his fist.

Eyes large with horror, Diana stared down numbly at the corpse she'd made. She was roused from her stupor when Bassity's body suddenly twitched violently in its death-throes, then was still. Unable to bring herself to pry the derringer from his firm grip, Diana fought back the nausea that threatened to overcome her and, shuddering at touching the body, dug the key from Bassity's vest pocket.

Fearing his eye might remain on her heel, Diana left the shoe in place. There was nothing of true worth amongst the strewn contents of her ruined reticule; besides she did not care to remain with the ghastly corpse any longer than necessary. Slipping her cape about her bare shoulders to hide her near-nakedness, she hobbled to the door, then paused, listening for sounds of Li. Deciding it was safe, Diana unlocked the door and stepped out.

The hall appeared empty. Determined to walk all the way to Percy Wilberforce's hotel, Diana rushed to the front door. She threw it open wide and ran outside, right into the waiting arms of Li and two hatchetmen with ropes.

Her startled cry was cut short as a wadded cloth was thrust into her red mouth and held in place by a second widely knotted cloth that was shoved between her teeth and tied viciously tight at the back of her head. Her madly struggling body was half-dragged, half-carried to a closed carriage and forced inside. The hatchetmen climbed in after her with their ropes, and Li took his place on the driver's box.

With a snap of the whip, Li set the team in motion. There was no traffic in the isolated area so he urged them into a canter, the carriage body swaying from side to side with the movement and the struggle inside as the two men tied Diana's resisting form hand and foot on the floor.

From his concealment in the shadows, Tony Gamble had witnessed Diana Logan's abduction. Incensed at the gall of the yellow-skinned, slant-eyed foreigners to dare lay a finger on a white woman, he wheeled his horse and set off at a gallop to gather the hoodlums and effect Diana's rescue – even if it meant burning and sacking all of Chinatown.

CHAPTER TWENTY

The bored desk clerk didn't even raise an eyebrow when Matt Sutton sloshed into the hotel and demanded his key. In his day he had probably seen others who had narrowly escaped being shanghaied. Leaving a soggy trail across the lobby, up the stairs, and along the hall, Matt went to his room. It was still in order, and, forcing the adjoining door open, he saw that Diana's room was too. Either Bassity wasn't on to her yet, or else she was to be taken from the saloon to Little Pete's harem.

Carrying her large water pitcher, he returned to his room, where he stripped off his wet clothing and emptied its contents over his head. He repeated the process with his own pitcher and further washed the grimy salt water of San Francisco Bay from his body, then dried himself with a towel.

Since he had been found out, there was no further reason to dress like a dude, so he put on his comfortable range clothes and strapped on his shell belt and six-gun. He felt better immediately in his fighting clothes and was ready to take on any and all bad men that San Francisco had to offer.

*

A half-hour later, Matt arrived at the employees' rear entrance to the Belle La Grande and was told curtly by a burly bouncer that Diana was not appearing that night. One of the passing saloon girls added enviously that Diana was spending the evening at Jake Bassity's house, which was a rare honour as only a few knew where it was located.

Disregarding the bouncer's gruff order to be on his way, Matt stood thoughtfully digesting what he'd learned. While it seemed logical that Jake Bassity would want a private evening with Diana, it was strange that he would pick a Saturday night, his saloon's biggest time, to deprive the customers of his star attraction. Matt had the uneasy feeling that there was more to it than merely a romantic evening on Jake Bassity's part. Then his thoughts were rudely intruded upon.

'Hey, cowboy, are you deaf?' the bouncer said harshly. With that he gave Matt a hard shove toward the door and pulled a blackjack from his coat. 'Git or I'll bust you up!'

Matt smiled disarmingly, then shot a quick left to the man's solar plexus, doubling him over gasping for air, then straightened him up with a solid uppercut. The man went down like a pole-axed steer. Satisfied, Matt turned and went out, leaving the saloon girl staring after him in opened-mouth surprise.

Deciding it was high time to inform Percy Wilberforce of the night's happenings and seek his help in finding Jake Bassity's house, Matt went around to the front of the Belle La Grande and hailed a hansom cab.

During the drive Matt fretted impatiently, hoping Bassity had not learned Diana was a spy, and that Wilberforce did indeed know how to find his house. Matt was so deep in thought that he paid little heed to the crowded street traffic except to regard it as an annoyance. He didn't even spare a second glance at a carriage, its curtains drawn, driven by an Oriental as it passed right by in the opposite direction and was unaware that Diana Logan lay tied and gagged on the floor at the feet of her two captors.

Diana Logan was equally unaware of Matt Sutton's passing cab as she lay gagged and roped from shoulders to crossed ankles in a taut hog-tie and completely shrouded by her cape. The sounds of pedestrians and horse-drawn conveyances served to magnify her sense of helplessness and frustration. Who would suspect that a captive blonde was hidden inside the carriage?

Hoping to prolong the feeling in her limbs, Diana went limp in her ropes. She realized grimly that with Matt shanghaied and Percy Wilberforce unaware of her predicament, it was up to her alone to help herself and somehow rescue Countess Arabella Stanton as well. At the moment it seemed an impossible task.

Refusing to give herself over to despair, Diana recalled that she had often been in dire situations during the lengthy journey to the Far West, but things had always worked out. Holding that thought, she tried to banish her tension and compose her badly strained nerves.

Diana had no idea how long the trip had taken before the carriage finally drew to a stop in a quiet area. With the sometimes snail's pace because of the noisy traffic, it had seemed interminable. Her tied, cramped body complained at being immobile for so long, and seconds had seemed minutes and minutes hours.

Diana tensed as the two men broke their stony silence and spoke back and forth in Chinese. The cape was jerked aside, and she blinked at the sliver of moonlight invading the darkened carriage from a crack in the drawn curtains. Before her eyes could adjust a man raised her to a sitting position by her shoulders, with her back against his seat, and blindfolded her deftly with a thickly folded cloth while the other man was heard climbing from the carriage.

Again wrapped in her cape to hide her ropes and scanty clothing, Diana was pulled out of the carriage by the second man and carried a short distance. The carriage door shut, and it drove away. The first man joined them, and Diana heard a door creak open. As she was carried inside, her bound feet brushed against the door frame and her remaining shoe was dislodged. It either fell to the floor unnoticed or else the men did not care, since they started up a flight of stairs without a pause.

By the second-floor landing the man carrying

Diana was winded and voiced his complaint. After a brief conference, Diana's legs and ankles were freed and she was set on her wobbly feet, then supported between the men up the remaining two long flights of stairs. Next they moved through what she guessed to be several large rooms that echoed with her captors' footsteps. At last they stopped and one of the men gave a short series of identifying raps on a door directly before them.

After a long moment Diana heard a heavy bolt being drawn back and the door opened inward. An older woman's voice spoke curtly in Chinese and the men replied as they guided Diana forward into the room. More words were exchanged, then the men left, their departing footfalls again kicking up echoes. Diana flinched involuntarily as the heavy door closed loudly behind her and the bolt was shot back into place. The older woman issued commands and two younger voices answered meekly in Chinese as the women hurried to Diana.

Gentle hands removed her cape and blindfold, and Diana winced at the unaccustomed brightness. The women started to free Diana from her ropes and gag, but a sharp word from the older woman stopped them instantly. Diana's blurred vision adjusted and she saw a tall, thin, sallow old hag in a black robe, with a large set of keys in the girdle of her waist, studying her nigh-naked figure from head to stockinged toes appraisingly. The ropes about her touching elbows pulled her shoulders back and forced her taut breasts to strain at the thin top of her torn chemise. The old woman nodded in satisfaction and her dark eyes bored into Diana's large blue ones.

'When you are allowed to speak you will address me at all times as "Old Mother",' she said austerely, 'in a most respectful tone of voice.' Diana only stared back unblinkingly. 'I am told it was your intention to free the English noblewoman from her life of luxury here.' She made a sweeping gesture about the very ornate, palace-like room with shiny gilt furniture, decorative murals, and wrought-iron lamps that cast animal and other patterns on the walls, floor and high ceiling. 'I wish her to see you helplessly bound and gagged, as she herself was first brought to us.' She smiled wickedly. 'Then she will realize once and for all that there is no escape and accept her lot, as you too will learn to do, my beautiful one.'

Though her eyes defiantly flashed blue lightning above her cheek-pinching gag, Diana knew the only thing to do was remain passive until she knew her way around the place. At the moment she did not even know if she was still in San Francisco.

Issuing a stern command in Chinese, Old Mother turned and led the way in a stately manner toward a yawning archway on the far side of the room. A young woman, in bright yellow tunic, trousers and slippers, took Diana's upper arm lightly but firmly and steered her after Old Mother while the similarly clad woman carrying her cape trailed meekly behind them.

At least she was on her way to finally meet Lady

Arabella Stanton. The circumstances were not as she had expected, but Diana refused to give up hope of their escape or rescue.

CHAPTER TWENTY-ONE

Percy Wilberforce was relaxing over a tall whiskey and soda at a corner table in the hotel bar and browsing over his notes with the names and dates of various politicians, besides several jockeys, meetings and acceptances of bribes from Little Pete and Jake Bassity. It would all make splendid reading in the newspaper.

Pleased, he closed his notebook and returned it to an inner breast-pocket of his suit. With pressure put on the higher circles of city government, action would have to be taken against Little Pete. Already the tongs, with the blessings of the mandarin from Hong Kong, had posted a placard prominently in Chinatown offering a reward for his death, and they were gearing up for a bloodbath. That was another reason that the Countess of Rossnere needed to be extracted from his harem as quickly as possible.

Reminding himself not to get headaches ahead of time and that he had two very capable operatives in the persons of Matt Sutton and Diana Logan, Wilberforce leaned back comfortably in his chair and took a long swallow of his drink, then gave a deep sigh of contentment. All was right with the world.

It was then that he saw Boggs, his face a portrait of solemnity, approaching urgently with a tall, equally sombre cowboy, whom he recognized as Matt Sutton. Wilberforce knew immediately that he was not going to like what they had to say. Sadly, all was no longer right with the world.

Diana Logan was conducted along a maze of winding corridors with various rooms on either side. At first she did her best to remember, in hopes of later retracing her route, but soon gave up in hopeless frustration and confusion. They came to an ornate set of doors that Old Mother pushed inward to reveal a large room where a group of Caucasian women, in various enticing Chinese outfits, lounged about on sofas and large pillows and broke off their conversations to stare with bovine expressions at the newcomer.

'Where is the English one?' Old Mother asked tersely.

The ten women exchanged glances, then one woman said, 'She's probably in her room.'

'Yeah,' another woman agreed. 'She don't favour associating with the likes of us peasants.'

Diana noted that while attractive, the women had a hardness to their features, and guessed that they had been little more than prostitutes before joining

Little Pete's harem. She also suspected that most had done so willingly. Long used to the jealousies of other women, Diana sensed that despite her dishevelled appearance the women were regarding her as a rival. She certainly did not need them interfering with her escape plans. Diana could feel their hostile eyes on her as she was led away and decided it would be very unwise to be in the same room with the women without Old Mother or servants present.

After passing several more doors they entered a room without knocking. A woman in a long, high-necked Chinese dress reclined on a sofa, reading by a lamp on an ornately carved table. She looked up from her book in annoyance, which changed quickly to surprise then curiosity at the sight of Diana.

'Old Mother,' she said coolly in a clipped British accent, 'I have asked you repeatedly to knock before entering my room.'

'A thousand pardons, "Ladyship",' Old Mother said caustically, 'but what I have here will be of much interest to you.' She paused, enjoying the woman's perplexity.

Diana saw that she was mid-twenties, auburn-haired, with hazel eyes and delicate, aristocratic features, exactly like the photograph that Percy Wilberforce had shown her when she and Matt had first agreed to work for him.

Old Mother was chagrined that the young woman refused the bait and remained silent, forcing her to continue unprompted. 'This woman and a man plotted your rescue,' she said, trying to keep the asperity from her tone, and was pleased to see a flicker of hope come over Lady Arabella's face. 'The man is now on a ship to South America. The woman has been brought here helpless, as you once were, to join the Master's house of women.' She relished the crestfallen expression on her victim's face and allowed the two women to exchange sympathetic looks.

Because of her situation Diana did not concern herself with protocol. To attempt to curtsy (something she had never done before) while tied and gagged would not only be awkward but ludicrous, especially if she fell flat on her face.

'You "ladies" may become acquainted later,' Old Mother purred deliciously. 'I am certain you will spend many long hours discussing your similar plight.' She waited but the noblewoman maintained her silence. 'This one must now be made presentable for the Master's gathering, to which you are not included this night.' With that she and the women left with Diana.

Lady Arabella Stanton, Countess of Rossnere, put aside her book and tried to rouse herself from the despondency induced by the despised old hag. She had almost given up hope that Hugh had survived his enforced South Seas voyage. If Old Mother was not playing a cruel jest for her own amusement (something she would not put past the woman), then he was alive and actively searching for her. She would learn more whenever she was able to talk with the young blonde. Perhaps she now had an ally, and together they could escape this hated place. Encouraged, but not allowing herself to build her hopes too high yet, Arabella tried to return to her book. It took some wilful concentration, but she slowly became once more immersed in the story.

Matt, Boggs, and Wilberforce were in a rattling carriage racing for Jake Bassity's house. Previously, Wilberforce had discreetly followed several politicians to their clandestine meetings there with Little Pete and the saloon owner. As the carriage came to a fast stop, they saw that the front door of the dark house stood wide open.

Wilberforce frowned, studying the house warily, 'I do not like the looks of this.'

'Me neither,' Matt seconded, and bolted out ahead of the others.

Telling the driver to wait, Wilberforce, accompanied by Boggs, followed Matt into the ominously silent house.

CHAPTER TWENTY-TWO

Hair and make-up immaculate (if not a bit gaudy), Diana, in gilded sandals and a snug, high neck, jade-green dress, a lengthy slit up one side that emphasized her tall, lithesome figure and long splendid legs, was brought to a huge dining-room where Little Pete, decked out in silks and sash like an Oriental potentate, and his henchmen were eating at a low table with selected Caucasian women while three petite dancing girls entertained to lilting music made by a small group of Chinese musicians. The stocky tong leader scrutinized her from blonde head to red-lacquered toes while chewing a bulging mouthful of food, and made appropriate noises of approval. He seized one of her slender wrists in a steely grip and pulled her down none too gently on a large cushion beside him. Her empty glass was filled with wine, while another male servant heaped her plate with meat, rice, and vegetables, then she was ordered to eat and drink.

To Diana's distress, the only utensils were chopsticks.

Displaying all the skill of an average Occidental, Diana sat picking at her food with the chopsticks. Concern over her present situation did not help her dexterity, and more food fell back on to her plate than reached her red mouth, much to the amusement of Little Pete and his entourage. She hated being watched while doing something that she did not do well, but she had not eaten since her light noon lunch.

'You will become used to chopsticks,' Little Pete said, nudging her ribs with an elbow, 'as you shall be with me for a long time.' He laughed, and the others joined in.

'How long is that?' Diana asked, dreading the answer.

He made an exaggerated face as he scowled thoughtfully, then shrugged broadly. 'Until I tire of you. Then maybe I will sell you to a pleasure house of women . . . or a very rich old man who likes white women.' Diana stared at him coldly. Little Pete merely laughed heartily and turned his attention back to the graceful dancers.

Since starving was out of the question, Diana put pride aside and, ignoring the men's smirking faces, concentrated on manipulating the maddening chopsticks. She was relieved when the group soon decided that the delicate, colourfully clad dancing girls were more entertaining, and she was left to eat in relative peace.

*

Armed with knives, sling-shots, and pistols, nearly a hundred hoodlums eager for an excuse to raise hell rallied behind Tony Gamble self-righteously in the noble crusade to save a blonde, Anglo-Saxon white woman from the evil hands of the heathen Chinese. The raucous, torch-lit parade descended upon Chinatown like a swarm of angry locust, wreaking havoc on individuals and businesses alike. The few policemen made a half-hearted attempt to disperse the mob, then beat a hasty retreat in search of reinforcements. Seeing the 'coppers' routed encouraged the hoodlums to even more devastation, and any 'Chinaman' not swift of foot was pummelled to the ground, kicked, and relieved of his pigtail.

Matt, Boggs, and Wilberforce stood staring down at Bassity's body, French-heeled shoe embedded to its hilt in his right eye and obscuring most of his bloody face. The bullwhip and Diana's torn clothing lay scattered about the large room, in silent testimony of the violence that had taken place.

'I should say the young lady was most justified in ridding San Francisco of one of the Barbary Coast's worst denizens,' Wilberforce remarked in admiration. 'And in such a novel way indeed.'

Matt motioned to the derringer clutched tightly in the dead man's hand. 'That's Diana's gun, so she didn't have many choices.'

'She is now most probably in Little Pete's harem. Have you succeeded in ascertaining where exactly that would be?'

'No, but I've a pretty good idea.'

'Then let us be on our way, post-haste,' Wilberforce said and led the way from the room.

'Please . . . not here in front of everyone . . .' Diana gasped, struggling, both hands shoving against Little Pete's thick chest, as she turned her head aside and shied from his aggressive hands seeking to envelop her in a drunken embrace.

With a heavy sigh of frustration, the tong leader sat back, glaring, then grabbed her wrist. 'Come now, and we shall be alone.' He stood and jerked Diana to her feet so hard she feared her slim arm would be dislocated at the shoulder. Heedless of her protests, he started to drag her away amid his underlings' laughter and amused remarks.

Diana tried to hang back, and aware that resistance was useless, raked his imprisoning hand with her sharp red nails. Little Pete yelled and loosened his grip, staring dumbly in surprise at the back of his hand as droplets of blood began to ooze from the thin red furrows across its length. Diana yanked her aching wrist free, the strong effort throwing her off balance. Before she could right herself and run, Little Pete growled in rage and lashed out with a savage backhand that caught her across the side of her face and resounded throughout the room. The force of the blow hurled Diana to the floor, seeing flares and pinwheels erupt before her dazed eyes and feeling her cheek throb hotly.

'If you do not wish to be with me,' Little Pete spat harshly, 'then you shall entertain all that are here.' He strode forward, seized a huge fistful of Diana's

149

tousled hair and dragged her agonizingly to her tottering feet, then thrust her out on to the now empty dancefloor. 'You take off your clothes slowly, a little at a time.' He ripped a shoulder of her high-necked dress, the shriek of the delicate material merging with Diana's own startled cry, and started to turn away.

'No,' Diana said in icy defiance and stood her ground, glowering back at him. The thought of disrobing slowly in front of the drunken men and women was abhorrent.

'It is time you learn you are nothing but a humble, insignificant slave who must always obey me!' Little Pete clapped his hands, the sound reverberating deafeningly in the large, now quiet room, and spewed a torrent of guttural commands to the servants milling about. Two men hastened away while two more rushed forward.

Diana gave a half-gasp, half-cry and struggled violently as the two men grabbed her arms and pulled her swiftly to a line of slender, decorative pillars on one side of the room. A servant returned with lengths of thin silken cord and tied her clasped hands tightly in front of her. Another cord cinched her bindings, then her arms were raised above her head, and the other end was wound around a post, fastening her against it on straining tiptoes, her back to the group. She cried out in distress as her dress was ripped savagely down the middle to her trim waist and spread wide to either side, baring her satiny, ivory flesh. Diana turned her head and cringed, eyes wide with fright, as she saw Little Pete take the handle of a cat-o'-nine-tails from the second returning servant.

'I enjoy making proud white women beg and crawl!' he hissed and grinned cruelly.

Diana shuddered involuntarily as he swiped the air viciously with the long lashes, their ends tiny knotted balls. She turned away quickly and buried her face in the inverted V of her upraised arms. She had never known true pain, not even a broken bone in childhood, and she doubted that she would bear it well. The thought of begging the hated tong leader's forgiveness and promising to obey his every demand flashed through her desperate mind, but a stubborn resolve kept her mute.

Biting her soft lower lip to hopefully avoid crying out, Diana steeled herself for the blow that would signal the beginning of her ordeal. This would be different than it had been earlier with Bassity. She was now tied and helpless to avoid any of the blows. Diana prayed urgently that Matt would find her. Then she remembered that he had supposedly been shanghaied aboard a ship bound for South America. She hoped earnestly he would somehow escape and come in search of her.

There was still Percy Wilberforce and his man Boggs. But would they know where to find her, and could they arrive in time to stop the terrible torture that was about to begin at any second?

CHAPTER
TWENTY-THREE

Chinatown was in chaos. Looting was widespread as the mob, strengthened by non-hoodlums who also seized the opportunity to make a 'fast buck' at the expense of the Chinese, raged through the streets. The loud clanging of bells announced the arrival of police wagons. Nightsticks flailing the coppers flew into the crowd and sought to halt the advancing tide. Again they were greatly outnumbered, and for every howling hellion beaten into submission a dozen took his place.

Unnoticed in the mêlée, Tony Gamble became a victim of his own making. Downed by a wildly thrown brick that cracked his skull, he fell and was trampled to death underneath the feet of the surging, battling horde.

Halted in the heavy traffic backed up around Chinatown, Matt, Boggs, and Wilberforce left their carriage and started off on foot for the shoe factory over a hundred yards ahead. Matt was surprised that, despite his size, Wilberforce was able to keep up.

As they neared the sprawling building they saw a group of Chinese with knives, hatchets and pistiols storming up the stairs. Then sounds of gunshots and battle cries merged with the distant noise of the riot in Chinatown.

'It appears the rival tongs have decided to use the distraction to do away with Little Pete and his tong,' Wilberforce said in between breaths and leaned heavily on his walking stick as they paused to survey the situation.

'I don't give a damn about him,' Matt said, 'but their attack places Diana and Countess Arabella in danger.'

'The rescue shouldn't be too complicated,' Boggs said lightly. 'We just shoot everyone who's not a woman.'

'Yeah,' Matt said and grinned. Then he led the way toward the building.

On reaching the stairs, the three saw a lone black French-heeled shoe and speculated that it belonged to Diana. 'We shall have the answer shortly,' Wilberforce said confidently, 'but I do believe you are right, Sutton.' Guns drawn, Matt and Boggs ascended the stairs ahead of Wilberforce and followed the sounds of bloody mayhem.

Slowly, deliberately stretching the suspense, for he knew the wait was far worse than the actual pain, Little Pete drew back his brawny arm and prepared to strike.

The blow never came.

Suddenly all hell broke loose outside. There were gunshots, dying screams, and frenzied voices.

Diana flinched, startled, and dared a look over her shoulder. The room was a scene of mass confusion. Servants, dancers, and musicians scattered in fright, as did the women at the long table. She saw her tormentor hurl the whip aside and shout a flurry of orders to his underlings as the deadly tumult outside intensified. She hoped her rescue was at hand, either by Percy Wilberforce and the authorities or, somehow, Matt Sutton. Even if the attackers were from a rival tong, she couldn't be any worse off than she was now.

A man came running in, his grimy appearance told that he had been in the midst of the fighting. He spoke hurriedly to Little Pete, who raged and shook his fists at the heavens, apparently cursing and calling down destruction on his attackers, as the savage fighting crept steadily nearer. He snatched one of the pistols from the man's double holster gunbelt then snarled guttural orders and stalked toward Diana while the man raced from the room.

Diana recoiled and tugged helplessly at her bonds. She had hoped the brawny man would forget about her in the chaos. Thrusting the pistol into his wide, bright sash, Little Pete withdrew a knife concealed there and deftly severed the cinch rope attaching Diana's tied wrists to the pillar. Discarding the knife ringingly across the floor, he took the end of the long cord and yanked Diana after him by her wrists toward a door at the far end of the large room. Brutal tugs on her wrists and outstretched arms (which she feared would be torn from their sockets) kept Diana from attempting to hold back as she ran stumblingly behind Little Pete, her sandals making dainty echoes with every step.

As they reached the heavy, ornate door, bursts of gunfire and men's dying shrieks erupted throughout the opposite hallway. Little Pete shoved the door open and hesitated to toss a wary look behind him. Diana turned and her face abruptly mirrored absolute surprise.

Crouched, smoking Colt held ready, Matt Sutton cautiously entered the room. His swift gaze swept the area and settled on Diana and Little Pete in the wide doorway. Recovering from his own surprise at seeing Matt, Little Pete jerked Diana against him by her wrists, using her as a shield, while his free hand clawed the six-gun from his sash. Diana's nearness prevented Matt from chancing a shot at the man, and he made a stretching leap for the shelter of the low table. He landed short and desperately rolled towards it. Diana's fearful scream was drowned by the deadly blast from Little Pete's pistol.

Slugs tore searchingly into the wood floor, kicking up a hail of thick splinters, as they chased after Matt's turning body. He reached the relative safety of the table and more slugs slammed into bowls, plates and glasses on its top, hurling their pieces, food, drink, and splinters madly in all directions. Matt stayed low, huddled between two large pillows, until the ear-rending echoes faded into silence.

Little by little Matt raised his head carefully and peered directly across the littered tabletop at the now empty doorway. Curbing his impatience, he forced himself to wait endless seconds to make sure it wasn't a ploy to catch him out in the open when he went for the doorway. He heaved a broken plate. It shattered into fragments loudly in the middle of the room, but brought no response from beyond the doorway. Gauging that it was safe, Matt leaped up and pounded to the door.

Flattening against the doorjamb, he listened to Diana's light sandals slapping the floor and the man's heavy footsteps disappearing along the hall. He peeked around the doorjamb just in time to see them start through a door at the end of the long corridor. Again he was unable to risk a shot and let the two exit before charging after them.

Outside the sounds of mayhem and disorder were even more frightening. But the mob's violence was almost spent, as without its leader there was no organized thought and it ran helter-skelter through the streets. The police nightsticks broke heads and limbs and drove the hoodlums into yammering, cussing retreat. Ambulances and paddy wagons were crammed to overflowing, and slowly a semblance of order was finally restored. At least, until a new incident, real or imagined, caused another rabble-rouser to incite a mob invasion of Chinatown for looting and destructive fun at the expense of the peaceful Chinese.

CHAPTER TWENTY-FOUR

Lady Arabella Stanton sat rigid on the sofa, listening nervously to the chilling sounds of violence out in the hall. She wished she were able to lock her door but the only lock was on the outside, so Old Mother could confine her in her room for any infraction of the strict rules governing the House of Women. She flinched and stared wide-eyed at the closed door as the frightened screams and babbling of the other women and the unintelligible male Chinese voices neared her room.

Suddenly the door was thrown open and a cruel-faced Chinese, bloody hatchet in hand, entered and approached, leering. Somehow Arabella found her voice and, trying to conceal her fear, ordered him sternly from the room. The man only continued towards her. She hurled her book but he jerked his head aside and it flew through the doorway and landed in the hall. Despite herself, Arabella gave in to the scream that rose in her throat as the man reached out a hand to grab her.

'You there, fellow,' a deep voice boomed. 'Stand away from that lady.'

Surprised, the man whirled, hatchet raised, and received the thick brass handle of a walking stick right across his face with the full weight of Percy Wilberforce's massive bulk. The terrific blow sent the man reeling across the room like a drunken ballerina. He smashed soundly into the wall and wilted to the floor in a bloody, unconscious heap.

'Please do forgive the quite necessary violence, your ladyship,' the fat man said and stepped to Arabella, who was regaining her composure. Smiling like a benign Buddha, he gave a polite nod and introduced himself. 'Lady Arabella, I am Percy Wilberforce, and I have been engaged by your husband to bring you home to Rossnere.'

Tension flowing from her slender body with her relieved sigh, Lady Arabella smiled graciously. 'Thank you, Mr Wilberforce.' She extended a hand to her rescuer.

Reaching the open door at the end of the corridor, Matt hesitated, shoving more shells into his Colt. Two sets of footsteps were hurrying down a flight of stairs. Matt ducked through the doorway and pressed against the shadowy wall.

Below, Diana and Little Pete reached a landing and paused to look up the stairwell. He raised his gun towards Matt, but Diana seized his arm and deflected the echoing shot. With an oath, he backhanded her away. She fell to the floor and almost rolled over the edge.

Matt was aware of Little Pete's chain mail, but the dim light made a head shot risky. In desperation, he fanned the Colt until it was empty.

The smashing impact of each rapid slug against his chain mail jolted Little Pete backwards, stiff-legged, a step at a time. Off balance, his foot missed the step below the landing and, gun discharging into the ceiling, he tumbled down the stairs at an angle. Gathering momentum, his wildly careening body slammed into a railing support post that broke under his forceful weight. He rolled out into the middle of the empty stairwell and swiftly fell, shriek-ing, gun firing and bringing down wood and plas-ter. His screams ended abruptly with the resound-ing crash of his body against the unyielding concrete floor.

Skull, neck, and other bones broken, Little Pete's body twitched madly in its death-throes, lifeless finger firing the final shot in his pistol, then lay still in a steadily widening pool of blood.

Grimly holstering his smoking Colt, Matt descended the stairs hurriedly to Diana. Kneeling, he drew her inert form safely away from the edge of the landing and gently brushed her long, dishev-elled hair back from her face. She gasped his name and, draping her tied wrists behind his neck, pressed her trembling body against his while murmuring little mindless words of love. Matt held her tightly and stilled her voice with his lips. Relishing each other's nearness, time and place were forgotten as they held the kiss and embrace.

Boggs, Lady Arabella, and Wilberforce emerged from the hall into the main room only seconds before Matt and Diana. With Little Pete's death, the remaining attacking hatchetmen withdrew, as did the women and servants. A safe there, and later another in Little Pete's apartment, presented no challenge to Boggs's talent as a cracksman, and yielded incriminating papers and ledgers that indisputably proved the corruption of the city councilmen whom Wilberforce was investigating.

Several days later, with their fee safely deposited in a reputable San Francisco bank, Matt and Diana were married, with Boggs best man, Countess Arabella Stanton bridesmaid, and Percy Wilberforce giving the bride away. The wedding and reception were attended by the mayor, his wife, and some of the city's most influential people.

'Bet you never thought we'd have such an impressive wedding did you?' Matt said and hugged Diana to him.

'Honestly, there were times when I thought we never would have a wedding, simple or impressive,' Diana said and snuggled against him.

'Well, our travelling days are done. We're in California to stay. The mayor told me about some good grazing land up north of here. We'll settle there and raise cattle and kids. How does that sound, Mrs Sutton?'

'Heavenly, Mr Sutton!'